G R JORDAN

Wild Swimming

A Highlands and Islands Detective Thriller #40

First edition

ISBN (print): 978-1-917497-10-7
ISBN (digital): 978-1-917497-09-1

This book was professionally typeset on Reedsy.
Find out more at reedsy.com

"Give me coffee to change the things I can, and the beach to accept the things I can't."

Contents

Foreword	iii
Acknowledgments	iv
Books by G R Jordan	v
Chapter 01	1
Chapter 02	12
Chapter 03	21
Chapter 04	31
Chapter 05	41
Chapter 06	50
Chapter 07	59
Chapter 08	69
Chapter 09	80
Chapter 10	89
Chapter 11	97
Chapter 12	106
Chapter 13	114
Chapter 14	123
Chapter 15	132
Chapter 16	140
Chapter 17	148
Chapter 18	157
Chapter 19	165
Chapter 20	174
Chapter 21	183

Chapter 22	191
Chapter 23	200
Chapter 24	208
Chapter 25	215
Read on to discover the Patrick Smythe series!	223
About the Author	226
Also by G R Jordan	228

Foreword

The events of this book, while based around real and also fictitious locations around Scotland, are entirely fictional and all characters do not represent any living or deceased person. All companies are fictitious representations. This novel is best read waist deep in the Scottish sea. But maybe sit in front of the fire with a hot toddy instead!

Acknowledgments

To Ken, Jean, Colin, Evelyn, John and Rosemary for your work in bringing this novel to completion, your time and effort is deeply appreciated.

Books by G R Jordan

The Highlands and Islands Detective series (Crime)

1. Water's Edge
2. The Bothy
3. The Horror Weekend
4. The Small Ferry
5. Dead at Third Man
6. The Pirate Club
7. A Personal Agenda
8. A Just Punishment
9. The Numerous Deaths of Santa Claus
10. Our Gated Community
11. The Satchel
12. Culhwch Alpha
13. Fair Market Value
14. The Coach Bomber
15. The Culling at Singing Sands
16. Where Justice Fails
17. The Cortado Club
18. Cleared to Die
19. Man Overboard!
20. Antisocial Behaviour
21. Rogues' Gallery
22. The Death of Macleod - Inferno Book 1

23. A Common Man - Inferno Book 2
24. A Sweeping Darkness - Inferno Book 3
25. Dormie 5
26. The First Minister - Past Mistakes Book 1
27. The Guilty Parties - Past Mistakes Book 2
28. Vengeance is Mine - Past Mistakes Book 3
29. Winter Slay Bells
30. Macleod's Cruise
31. Scrambled Eggs
32. The Esoteric Tear
33. A Rock 'n' Roll Murder
34. The Slaughterhouse
35. Boomtown
36. The Absent Sculptor
37. A Trip to Rome
38. A Time to Rest
39. Cinderella's Carriage
40. Wild Swimming
41. The Wrong Man (releasing 2025)
42. Drop Like Flies (releasing 2025)
43. Someone Else's Ritual (releasing 2025)
44. None Too Precious (releasing 2025)
45. Save the King (releasing 2025)
46. The Silent War (releasing 2025)

Kirsten Stewart Thrillers (Thriller)

1. A Shot at Democracy
2. The Hunted Child
3. The Express Wishes of Mr MacIver
4. The Nationalist Express
5. The Hunt for 'Red Anna'
6. The Execution of Celebrity
7. The Man Everyone Wanted
8. Busman's Holiday
9. A Personal Favour
10. Infiltrator
11. Implosion
12. Traitor

Jac Moonshine Thrillers

1. Jac's Revenge
2. Jac for the People
3. Jac the Pariah

Siobhan Duffy Mysteries

1. A Giant Killing
2. Death of the Witch
3. The Bloodied Hands
4. A Hermit's Death

The Contessa Munroe Mysteries (Cozy Mystery)

1. Corpse Reviver
2. Frostbite
3. Cobra's Fang

The Patrick Smythe Series (Crime)

1. The Disappearance of Russell Hadleigh
2. The Graves of Calgary Bay
3. The Fairy Pools Gathering

Austerley & Kirkgordon Series (Fantasy)

1. Crescendo!
2. The Darkness at Dillingham
3. Dagon's Revenge
4. Ship of Doom

Supernatural and Elder Threat Assessment Agency (SETAA)
Series (Fantasy)

1. Scarlett O'Meara: Beastmaster

Island Adventures Series (Cosy Fantasy Adventure)

1. Surface Tensions

Dark Wen Series (Horror Fantasy)

1. The Blasphemous Welcome
2. The Demon's Chalice

Chapter 01

'Hey Bic, did you get your old man's booze?'

Bic gave a broad grin as he held up a bulging rucksack. 'It's all in here. Got the lot. I'm dead if he finds out, though.'

'You'll be too drunk to notice anyway,' said Jimbo.

Jimbo was wearing a large jumper over a pair of tracksuit bottoms. It was cold, but he didn't care. They'd be all right once they got round. All they had to do was to get away from Sandside Bay, overlooked by the small hamlet of Fresgoe.

It was dark with no one around. The middle of winter. What could go wrong?

Jimbo had scoped it out over the previous weeks. There was a sea cave you could gain access to, if you went at the right time. If the sea was too choppy, it was awkward to get in, but with the smallest boat, they could just about manage it. The *smallest* boat had been acquired two weeks before and hidden in the grass.

It was an old craft that no one was using and was now stored far enough from the road that no one bothered with it. Tonight, the boys had gone there, picked the boat up on their shoulders and walked it down to the bay. The boat was now turned up the right way and bobbing on the edge of the tide.

'We need to get a move on,' said Lorry.

He was the youngest of them and, really, shouldn't have been contemplating drinking at all. Not that any of the others were particularly of an age. Cheeks had just reached that point where he could go in and get his drink legally. The others, not so. Also in the boat were several sleeping bags, a large bag of logs, a couple of pans, and packs of sausages and bacon.

'So what's your old man say, Bic? Has he gone for the weekend?'

'He's always gone,' Bic spat back. 'I don't talk about him, anyway.'

'No,' said Jimbo. 'Let's talk about your mother.'

Bic hit him on the shoulder. 'You don't talk about her that way either.'

'It's not Jimbo's fault,' said Cheeks. 'Bic, you've got the hottest mum of the lot of us.'

'You don't talk about her like that.'

'I don't want to talk to her,' said Jimbo.

Bic gave him a proper shove, sending him backwards, and he tipped over into the boat.

'Don't be like that,' said Cheeks. 'Anyway, we'd better get going. Don't want to make too much noise here.'

The boat was now loaded, and three of the boys got in while Bic pushed it out into the water, before jumping in himself. The oars were put out, and they rowed round the coast, hugging tight to it. As the boat bobbed up and down, Lorry looked the worse for wear because of it.

'It's a ruddy calm night,' said Cheeks. 'What are you getting all worked up about?'

'Let's just get there, okay? Let's just get there. Get this booze

2

down us,' said Lorry.

'Have you got anything else?' asked Bic.

'Of course I've got something else. We've got our vapes. We've got a few cigs here as well.'

'Good,' said Jimbo. 'We'll get this fire going too.'

'It's quite a high tide tonight though,' said Lorry. 'You sure there's going to be enough room in the cave?'

'You can sleep in the damn boat then, if there isn't,' said Cheeks. 'I know where I'm going.'

'I meant for a fire. If we don't get a fire going, we'll bloody freeze,' said Lorry.

'Stop complaining,' said Cheeks. 'What about this? What about that?'

'Shush,' said Bic, 'going along the coast. Don't want anyone to see us, do we? But once we're in the cave, they're not going to hear us.'

It was a dark night. Moonless. And it was extremely cold. The air was crisp, and apart from the sea gently lapping up against the rocks on the shore, occasionally hitting the boat, there was little else to hear. Occasionally, you could hear a car in the distance, but here on the north end of Scotland, you don't get that many people going about, not at this time of night. The bay had been completely dead. It was perfect for the boys. Finally a chance just to get away and do what the hell they wanted. No one else there.

It was twenty minutes before the sea cave appeared, almost lost in the dark. Bic pulled out his mobile phone, switched on the flashlight, and guided the boat gently in. It just about fitted through the entrance before the cave opened up. On either side there were ledges, almost like platforms.

Jumping up on one, Cheeks pulled the boat until it was fixed tight in. Beyond it, the rock formation opened up again, and the water went deep into the cave. The squeeze from the cave's interior would keep the boat fast and give them a point at which they could cross from one side of the rock formations to the other.

'Over here,' said Bic. 'We should put the fire here. You won't see it much from outside, and it's close enough that the smoke will vent away.'

'You get it going then,' said Cheeks. 'Let's start getting this booze out.'

On the other side of Bic, Cheeks unloaded the various bottles and beer that they'd brought with them. He cracked open a can, turned round and handed it to Jimbo, and then did three more, one for each of the rest of them. Bic had arranged a large number of firelighters underneath wood logs, struck a match, and set the fire going. He put his hands up to it.

'Bloody cold!'

'Who cares if it's cold? Get that beer down you. You won't feel it then, will you?'

Two hours later, the fire was blazing away, and the boys were feeling the heat from it. They'd guessed right and, cocooned in this little cave, they didn't feel cold. What they did feel was immensely happy, for the beer had been flowing and now the harder liquor was being consumed.

'What's the deal with you and Emma?' said Bic, looking over at Cheeks.

'Well, you know, women just can't resist me, can they?' said Cheeks.

Jimbo threw an empty can at him. 'You're an arsehole,' he said.

'Yeah, but she likes this arsehole,' said Cheeks.

Bic looked across at Lorry. 'You all right?' he said. 'Lorry, you all right?' Lorry was looking like he was about to vomit.

'Course I'm fine,' said Lorry, and then almost half fell backwards.

'If you're going to be sick,' said Cheeks, 'be sick in the water. Don't you dare puke up—.'

'Don't be sick in the water,' said Bic. 'That'll be lapping up everywhere.'

'It'll stink,' said Jimbo. 'If you're going to be sick, get to the back of the cave, all right? Puke up in there.'

'Maybe puke out the front,' said Cheeks.

'No. If he goes out there, he'll get woozy, and he'll fall in the water. I'll have to call for somebody. I'm not calling for somebody tonight. They'll bloody kill me. Anyway,' said Bic, 'did she let you do photos?'

'What?' asked Cheeks.

'Does that Emma let you do photos? You know, like the saucy ones, the good ones? She pose for you?' asked Bic.

'As if I'm going to show you if she did.'

'Oh, you would do. I mean, it's for the boys, isn't it? We're not telling. You'd have to send us copies, though.'

Cheeks threw a can over at Bic. 'You are one dirty sod, you know that? She is nice, though. I mean, really nice.'

'Yeah? What's she like, then?' asked Bic.

Cheeks grinned. 'Well, once you get her top off, you see she's . . .'

Lorry stood up suddenly. He jumped across the boat to the other side, making it crack loudly.

'Easy, arsehole,' said Bic. But Lorry was gone, falling over towards the back of the cave.

'You want to make sure he's all right?' asked Jimbo to the

others.

'Why do I have to make sure he's all right?' said Bic. 'I'm beside the ruddy fire. I'm keeping the fire going.'

'But me and Cheeks are on this side,' said Jimbo. 'He's on your side now.'

'Anyway, the eggs—are we going to keep them for the morning?' said Bic.

'Have a look at him. If he ends up falling in or something, we're up to our neck in it.'

'It's not my fault he can't handle his booze,' said Bic.

'Just make sure he's all right,' said Jimbo.

Bic shook his head, but he stood up from the fire and walked along the ledge further into the cave. It started to narrow, and he saw Lorry on his knees, vomiting hard up against the wall.

'Oh, for goodness' sake,' said Bic. 'He's puking his guts out.'

'Bloody pathetic,' said Cheeks.

'Make sure he's all right,' said Jimbo.

'Why me?'

'Because you're there,' said Jimbo. 'Get him back, stick him in a sleeping bag. What we can't have him doing, is falling in anywhere.'

Bic walked up behind Lorry and started hitting him hard on the back. Lorry vomited again and Bic stepped back quickly, eager not to get caught in any splashes.

'This is disgusting,' said Bic. 'How come I'm getting stuck with this? How come it's me?'

'Shut up,' said Jimbo. Bic could hear him getting up, heard his foot step into the boat, then onto the other side, but Bic also heard the crack of another can being opened.

He turned to see Jimbo, handing him a can. 'Here, get that down you. Wise up the little arsehole.'

'Shut up,' said Lorry, almost gasping between vomiting. He reached up and snatched Jimbo's drink off him and chugged a bit more beer before giving it back.

Jimbo put it down to one side. 'There's puke around the top of it now,' he said.

'I told you I'm fine,' said Lorry.

He vomited again.

'There's a sleeping bag out there,' said Jimbo. 'I think we want to put him in it. Make sure he's stowed away to one side safely, so he doesn't fall down into the water.'

'Leave him in the boat,' said Bic. 'Can't get out of the boat. Can't roll out of it.'

'It's not a bad idea,' said Jimbo. 'Anyway, come on.' He lifted Lorry up, but Lorry struggled, stumbled forward, and reached up, his hand grabbing hold of something in the dark.

'What? What is . . .' muttered Lorry as he felt something move.

Something fell and hit Lorry. He tumbled backwards into Jimbo and Bic, causing them both to stumble back.

Lorry's backside hit the cold floor as, in front of him, a figure fell, hit the rock side, and then tumbled into the water.

'What the hell's that?' said Lorry. 'What the hell?'

Bic stood like a statue. 'Jimbo? That was a . . .'

'That was a man. I'm sure that was a face,' said Jimbo.

'What the hell are you talking about?' shouted Cheeks from further back in the cave.

'Get the phone. Get your phone or something,' said Jimbo. 'We need to have a look.'

'I've got mine,' said Bic. He reached into his pocket, pulled out his phone, switching on the flashlight. He scanned it into the dark ahead. There was nothing. He swung it across the

7

water, in between the two ledges, and further into the back of the cave. As he did so, he stopped for a moment. A face looked back at them from the water. Bic shrieked, the phone dropping from his hands.

'What the hell?' said Lorry. He turned, struggling to get back, running as hard as he could to the front of the cave. He tumbled and rolled over, landing on the boat. Cheeks was up on his feet.

'What's going on back there?' he said.

'There's a bloody body,' said Bic. 'There's a pissing body in there.'

'You're taking the piss out of me,' said Cheeks. 'Quit it.'

'He's right,' said Jimbo. 'There's a bloody body in there.'

'Where?' said Cheeks.

Bic picked up his phone, shining the light into the dark recesses again. As Cheeks joined them, they looked down at the water, but there was nothing there. Meanwhile, Lorry was on his knees in the boat. He could feel the compulsion to vomit again, and had leaned over the edge of the boat, looking down into the water. However, as he did so, he felt an overwhelming surge within his stomach.

At the same time, a face appeared from underneath the boat working its way out towards the cave entrance. It was barely below the water, and in the firelight Lorry could see the face clearly. With every ounce of strength, he threw himself backwards in the boat.

'There!' he shouted. 'It's there! God! No!'

Cheeks turned, ran down to the boat, and found Lorry now on his backside, scrabbling away from the front end of it, the one that was nearest the cave entrance. From there, Cheeks looked into the water. He could see it, a body slipping out of the cave entrance.

'Where the hell?' blurted Bic.

'Is he alive?' said Cheeks.

'Lorry,' cried Jimbo, 'was that man alive?'

'How the hell should I know? How the hell?' Lorry was shaking now, violently. 'We need to go,' said Lorry. 'We need to get out of here. We need to go. We need to . . .'

'Calm down,' said Cheeks. 'Calm down.' Cheeks said to Jimbo, 'Was that guy alive?'

'I don't know. I mean . . . why would he be alive in here? Why would he be stuck up somewhere like that and be alive?'

'Maybe he was camping out like we were,' said Cheeks. 'Maybe he was . . .'

'What? Camping out?' said Jimbo. 'And we come in here, make all this racket, get pissed, and he just stays up there?'

'Maybe he's foreign,' said Cheeks. 'Maybe he was scared. Maybe he didn't want to step out with the four of us here.'

Jimbo looked at him. 'Get a grip.'

'But if he's dead,' said Bic, 'why would he be dead? Who would put him there? Was he . . .'

'He was naked,' said Lorry. 'When he came past, he was naked.'

'Hell,' said Cheeks.

'What do we do?' said Bic. 'What do we do? I can't phone people. Look at us. We're all out here with all this booze and everything. Where—'

'It's a dead person,' said Cheeks. 'There's somebody dead out here. I mean . . . it's the right thing. It's the right thing to do, isn't it?'

'If somebody's put him here, if he's naked and been put here,' said Jimbo, 'it means they could be watching the cave. They

9

could be spying. We could . . .'

'Can't tell them. Can't tell anyone,' said Lorry. 'I'll get into so much trouble. They're all . . .'

'Pissed is going to be the least of our problems,' said Cheeks. 'They're not going to give a toss if we're pissed. If we don't tell anyone, whoever's watching this could have seen us. They could come after us. We could be in trouble. But we tell people, at least then they know they'll look after us, yeah? They'll . . .'

'Well, why don't I go round and get help then?' said Jimbo.

'You're not leaving us in here,' said Bic. 'There's no way you're leaving us in here.'

'Then we all go,' said Cheeks. 'We stick together. Just in case somebody comes. Just in case.'

'What about the beer and that? Do we just, like, throw it in the sea?' said Jimbo.

'They won't care less about the beer. They won't care less about this. Just care about that body.' Cheeks looked around them. A fun night had just turned into a night from hell. But they couldn't cover it up, could they? And if it was discovered the body had been here, and they were here, could they get in trouble for it?

'So we go,' said Jimbo. 'We go.'

'We go,' said Cheeks. He looked around the cave one more time. He'd told the boys about this a month ago. His original plan had been to bring Emma out, but Emma had said no. Emma didn't like the idea of being out here in the cold. She didn't believe him. The fire would have worked. Maybe he'd been fortunate. How would Emma have reacted with a dead body falling down in front of him? He was not sure that she would have stuck around with him for long.

'I'll grab what I can,' said Jimbo, taking some of the booze.

'We'll throw it ashore somewhere. Come back for it later.'

'Let's just go,' said Cheeks. 'In case they're watching.'

Lorry sat at the back of the boat, not moving now.

'Push it off, Bic. Come on,' said Cheeks, getting into the boat. 'We need to find the police.'

Chapter 02

Alan Ross stood looking out at the sea. Not that often he got right up to the north of Scotland. Beyond this were Orkney and Shetland, but this was the end of the mainland. It was the sea for as far as he could care to look, but what he did see was an orange lifeboat making its way back and forward across the waves.

There was a Coastguard helicopter, too. Other fishing boats were moving back and forward in a search that had begun in the early hours of the morning. Now, at ten o'clock, Alan wondered if it was ever going to be successful. He'd been woken up to reports that a man's body was now out at sea.

The man was described as being naked and probably was almost certainly dead. He'd last been seen in a sea cave, and Susan Cunningham, freshly back from having her prosthetic leg fixed, had raced up to the north coast to meet up with the search coordinators. Ross had picked up Perry around about five in the morning from the station.

Hope McGrath, their DI, was having a few days off with her partner, John. Ross didn't begrudge her it, for she was going to become a mum. He understood life with kids as a father, now being a dad. He felt he had a better connection with parents, something he'd never really thought about. But he almost had a kinship with Hope. She had asked him several things in the office about how he had prepped for his arrival. But, of course. his arrival was much older when it arrived. For Alan and his partner certainly wouldn't be delivering any babies.

He had thought about contacting Macleod, but in truth, that would come. And Macleod would probably be on the phone soon. He was perhaps waiting to give Ross a chance to collect all the information.

'Then he would call. He'd make sure Ross was on top of it, to see if he needed to come out.'

'They're ready for you,' said Perry.

Ross nodded, turned and followed Perry across to a community building. It was fairly plain, but it had a few rooms inside. The heating had been put on by some kind caretaker, and inside sat four young men. There were blankets around them, and in truth, some of them looked the worst for wear.

'Have their parents arrived?' asked Ross.

'The ones we could find. I've got some officers to stand with them.'

'How are they, the boys?' asked Ross.

'A bit hung over. Lorry's looking very pale, a bit frightened to be honest,' said Perry. 'I think they were out for a bit of a laugh from what I can gather.'

'Is Jona here yet?'

'Yes, she's been setting up. She's trying to work out the best way to get into that cave. Nobody's been in it yet except for, I think, one of the RNLI guys. They just wanted to check, make sure the body wasn't still in the water in there.'

'Very good,' said Ross. He followed Perry into a room where four boys were sitting together on a sofa. Ross introduced himself to the boys and to the parents that had gathered, sitting on a sofa across from them.

'I'm Detective Sergeant Alan Ross. You've met Detective Constable Warren Perry. We're investigating the incident. I believe that we have a body. We don't know if it's suspicious or not yet. So, I'm just going to talk to the boys, see what they know.'

'It wasn't us,' said one boy.

'This is Cheeks,' said Perry.

'You prefer those names, do you?' asked Ross.

'Yes,' said Cheeks, 'but it wasn't us.'

'I didn't really think it was you,' said Ross. 'Very few people would do that sort of thing and then come and tell us. But I do need to know what was going on and what happened. So who have I got? You're Cheeks. You are . . .' He pointed at a bigger one of the lads.

'I'm Jimbo,' said the boy. They all had neatly trimmed hair, but Jimbo almost had the beginnings of a beard. The rest of them looked much fairer in the face.

Beside him was the whitest looking one.

'This is Lorry,' said Jimbo, 'he's not very well, and that's Bic on the end.'

'Bic?' said Ross.

'Did you see his collection of pens?' said Cheeks. Bic glared over.

'So tell me what you were doing.'

'Went out for the night,' said Cheeks. 'We're going to have a campfire, just have a bit of fun, a bit of booze, make our breakfast in the morning, come back.'

'You didn't tell me where you were going, you little shite!' said a woman.

'And you are?' asked Ross.

'Mrs Crexon,' said Perry.

'I'm his mother. And see when he gets home, he is in trouble. He's going to be—'

'Can we just stop with the threats?' said Ross. 'Your boys here have been through quite a shock. You may not like what they've done or where they've been, but they've done the right thing. They've come and reported something nasty. I need to pull as much information from them as possible. So please, can I just talk to them? When they go home, take it easy with them, okay? They've been through a real shock.'

Jimbo almost smiled at Ross. Ross wasn't sure that if it was his child that had done this, that he wouldn't take him home and give him the rounds of the kitchen. But the rounds of the kitchen in this little room would not help Ross's investigation.

'We got some booze together,' said Cheeks. 'Also, we got some sausages, bacon, firewood. We got a boat, took the boat round to a cave from here.'

'Where'd you get the boat?' asked Perry.

'It sits round in the marina. We're going to take it back, but it's been gone for a week and nobody's noticed.'

'You bloody took a boat!' said the woman that had spoken before.

Ross put his hand up to her. 'It's not relevant at the moment,' he said. 'So, you went round—?'

'We went round in the boat with all the stuff. I've been in that cave before,' said Cheeks suddenly. 'It's fantastic. There are a couple of ledges. The boat was the right size, you could jam it in. We were perfectly safe. We had a fire going and everything. Had some drinks.'

'Okay,' said Ross. 'Putting aside that you're getting yourself

15

intoxicated in a dangerous environment that you can't get out of easily, certainly not if you were drunk. But that aside,' said Ross, 'you're there, and what happens?'

'Well, Lorry can't hold his booze,' said Bic.

Lorry went to protest, but he was so white and ill-looking, it was completely in vain.

'He went to the back of the cave,' said Jimbo. 'He started to puke and that, so I said to Bic to go and look after him.'

'Which I did,' said Bic.

'I came to help him as well,' said Jimbo. 'We were picking Lorry up to try to bring him back to the fire. Going to put him in his sleeping bag and see if he could just go off to sleep, possibly in the boat. And then, well, then . . .'

'The body fell down,' said Lorry. 'It fell down in front of me.'

'Easy,' said Ross. 'Easy. What happened?'

'This body just falls down from up above us,' said Jimbo. 'I don't know if it was wedged or what, but Lorry put his hands up. He must have disturbed something because this body just fell down and it tumbles into the water. But at the time, well . . .'

'At the time we didn't realise it was definitely a body,' said Bic. 'We got our torches on, looking for it in the water. We couldn't find it.'

'That's when I came over,' said Cheeks. 'But we got Lorry into the boat. Or rather, Lorry sort of ended up in the boat. And then he . . .'

'What happened after that?' asked Ross.

'When did you see the face?' said Cheeks.

Lorry's head was still down. He seemed to shiver. It wasn't cold in the room anymore.

'I was going to throw up again,' said Lorry rather hoarsely.

16

'And then the face just . . . the face just . . .' He suddenly burst into tears. The other boys didn't berate him. They just looked at him.

'Who's . . . who's Lorry's parents?' said Ross.

A woman stood up and walked over. Lorry got out of the chair and she held on to him.

'It drifted out,' said Cheeks. 'The body drifted out. That's when we got on the boat and we came back.'

'Why did you come back?' asked Ross.

'Because it's the right thing to do.'

'You weren't worried you'd get in trouble then?' said Ross. 'You weren't worried that you might have disturbed the dead body and somebody else might know of that cave and might actually have seen you?'

'That's exactly what we thought,' said Jimbo. 'Look, we didn't do it immediately. We had a discussion for a few minutes. But, yeah, we came back to report it because . . . well, we didn't know if somebody was watching the place, did we?'

'You did the right thing,' said Ross. 'You should have reported, anyway. But you're right. You have no idea if anybody else is watching that place. You do not know about what they do or if they'll be looking out for you. So, you did the right thing.'

'Who is he?' said Lorry suddenly. 'Do you know who he is?'

His mother held him tight. The boy was still shaking.

'We need to get you to the paramedics again,' said Ross. 'Perry, get on the blower.'

Perry left the room. Ross looked over.

'Who was he?' said Jimbo.

'Well, if we find him, we might be able to work that out,' said Ross. 'They're searching for him at the moment.'

* * *

Susan Cunningham stood on the shore. There'd been a call. The helicopter had spotted something, and the lifeboat was moving towards it. She wasn't sure on the statistics of whether people would float, how long they could be alive for. She didn't reckon that somebody who had seemed dead when they went into the water, was naked, and out in these seas, could be alive.

She certainly wasn't hopeful. They'd been called because the boys had reported it as a dead body. Well, soon they'd find out. She picked up the phone and sent a text to Ross telling him she believed the body had been found. They were going to bring it into the nearest quay, and Susan had gathered along with an ambulance and others of the search group.

On the radio, the lifeboat said they'd picked up the body and were bringing it in. They confirmed they'd rendezvoused with the helicopter, the winchman having descended and confirmed that life was extinct. The winchman had since departed back up to the helicopter, and the lifeboat was on its way in.

It was an impressive orange vessel, but those on board were quiet, almost sombre. Susan watched as they tied up with ropes before bringing a body bag ashore and setting it down on the quayside.

Jona was over her shoulder, coming forward. She was dressed in her forensic gear and was holding everyone else back at a distance now. One of her colleagues was talking to the RNLI people, advising they needed the names of all those on board, just in case they had any DNA issues.

Jona unzipped the bag, pulling it back gently, looking down.

'Can I come near?' asked Susan.

Jona nodded and Susan broke the ranks of everyone else

watching to come up close. She stood a few feet away, not wanting to get too near the body as she wasn't suited up. Beside Jona, Cranston, a forensic photographer, was taking pictures of the face.

'Bloody hell,' said Susan.

'What?' said Jona.

'Do you not recognise him?'

'No,' said Jona.

There was a bit of commotion, and Susan turned to see Ross arriving. He strode through the gathered throng, telling them to stay back, and crept up towards Susan slowly.

'Am I okay here?' he asked Jona.

Jona nodded. 'We'll get the guy back to the mortuary and give you a bit more about it. But he's definitely deceased. I don't know how yet, obviously.'

'No, she doesn't,' said Susan, 'but I know who he is.'

'Who?' asked Ross.

'That's Stephen Ludlow. He was a UK open water swimming champion. He's driving an open water surge. People everywhere are opening up clubs. Wild swimming, they call it. These clubs are all tied to his business.'

'Is he well known, then?'

'He's off to get a knighthood in a week's time. I mean, he's been on telly with these clubs. You not seen the ads?'

'When do I get to watch telly these days?' said Ross. 'Stephen Ludlow, you say? Public figure, then?' he said quietly.

'Oh, yeah,' said Susan. 'Public figure. Press will be onto this one.'

Ross looked over at Jona and said quietly, 'Do you think it's foul play?'

'Alan, he's naked in a cave. A remote cave. It's not like he's a hermit that's gone wrong.'

'He's setting up all these clubs,' said Susan. 'And suddenly he's out of the way, dead and naked. The press will love this.'

'Okay,' said Ross. 'Jona, take him back and do your stuff. Tell me how he died.' He stood up, stepped back a few paces, then waved Perry over.

Susan joined the group.

'Right you two,' said Ross. 'We've got a dead man who's going to get a knighthood next week. I want to know why he's here, what he's doing in this part of the world, and how he ended up in a cave. Get into the hotels. See if he's been staying anywhere. See if he hasn't checked back.'

'Will do,' said Susan.

'Perry, his business is, apparently, open water swimming. Susan's just said he was opening up clubs, advertising them. See if there're any clubs along here. Might be why he was up. That would be a reasonable premise.'

Perry nodded. 'What are you going to do?'

'Well, given the nature of what happened and the fact he was going to get a knighthood, I think it's time to call in the big boss. I'm not covering off the press on this one,' said Ross.

'He's going to love you,' said Perry, almost giving a chortle, as he turned away.

Ross didn't like that. Macleod wasn't that way. Macleod would be here and he'd be professional. He picked up the phone and placed a call into the station. He was sure that Macleod would be happy; after all, he'd found the body that started the process. Now he needed to come and take charge.

Chapter 03

J ona Nakamura washed her hands. It was one of the easier examinations she'd done. Thankfully, the body hadn't been in the water that long, and the cause of death had been easy to establish. Now she would have to talk to Macleod about it. She'd managed to get her team into the cave but had travelled all the way back to Inverness herself to do the examination.

In a way, she was glad because the last thing she wanted to do was get on a boat to go round into that cave. It was a tough place to work in, and they were sweeping it as best they could. She had spent a half hour being debriefed by her number two. She didn't like the team being split like this. Jona always wanted to be at the front but she'd wanted a proper look at the cadaver.

She was still awaiting some toxicology reports, but she didn't think there would be anything in the system. It looked like a straightforward killing: brutal but clean.

After drying her hands, Jona got her gear together and threw the small rucksack over her shoulder. She walked through the station, and up the steps to Macleod's office.

The secretary gave a nod, indicating that the man was free.

As Jona approached, she knocked sharply on the door.

'Come in,' said a voice on the other side. Jona opened and saw Macleod messing about with his computer. Macleod was looking at Macleod.

'How do I make Ross come on that screen there so we can both see him?' said Macleod.

'Would you get yourself on a course,' said Jona.

Macleod frowned back at her, and then he grinned. 'I didn't work this long in the force,' he said, 'to not have people look after my technical deficiencies.'

'Have you got me coffee? I'm not doing it unless there's coffee,' said Jona, smiling.

'There's always coffee for you,' said Macleod.

'Well, go get it then,' she said.

Macleod stood up and walked out of his office, while Jona slid behind his desk. Soon, the screen on the left-hand side of the office had Ross's face on it, though frozen in image. Ross had put up a holding screen until Macleod had actually sorted out what he was doing. Ross wouldn't enjoy being watched on the other side while he waited.

'I've got it done on this side, Alan.'

'Jona,' he said, and suddenly the screen came to life. 'Don't tell me he had to get you to do it again. I sent him details. I sent him a whole thing explaining how to do this.'

'Do you mean the idiot's guide you sent through?'

'Yes, the idiot's guide,' said Ross. And then he stopped, realising Macleod had entered. 'Not that you're an idiot, sir.' Ross noticed Macleod was carrying two coffees.

'I thought you had somebody to do that,' said Ross.

'Ross, I'm able to get the coffees, okay? Stop treating me like I'm some sort of hallowed figure.'

'Yes, sir,' said Ross. Macleod shook his head, understanding he was off camera, before he sat down in front of a small table, placing a coffee down on it and calling Jona over.

'Just wait a minute. I need to switch the cameras, Alan. He wants to sit over there.'

Macleod gave a look over. 'He?' he said.

'I don't want to be too formal,' said Jona, smiling. She sat down beside him, and Macleod looked at the screen, smiling at Ross.

'Right then,' he said, 'so we've got a body found in the water, or rather in a cave, by a bunch of teenagers, and it hits the water and we've now picked it out. It is . . .?'

'Stephen Ludlow,' said Ross. 'He was a former UK open water swimming champion. He's been on the telly loads at the moment, driving the wild swimming phenomenon. He's been opening up clubs all around the country on a franchise basis. We believe he may have been up here doing that. I've got Perry looking into that. Susan's scanning the hotels, trying to find out where he's been.'

'Good,' said Macleod. 'Get his history. That's the first thing.'

'Who he is will cause a problem. He was up to receive a knighthood in a week's time,' said Ross.

'A knighthood?' said Macleod.

'I'm afraid so, sir. The press have already . . . , well, I've had a few calls; obviously, I've diverted them away.'

'Well, we'll need to get on top of that, then.'

'Can I ask, are you calling Hope back in?' asked Ross.

'No, Hope's off with John, and no, there are certain things that she can't come away from at the moment, that she needs to be there for, but that's okay. I'll run the case. You need to hold it together up there until I get there, probably at the end

23

of the day. What do we know about the cave?' asked Macleod.

'Well, you tell him,' Ross said to Jona. 'Your people were in it. I haven't even got near it yet.'

'It's difficult to access,' said Jona. 'We had to take a boat round, and a small boat at that. The RNLI got us inside in one of their—what do they call it—a Y-boat. It's like a very small RIB, sits on the back of the lifeboat. The team have been in, but it's difficult going. I'm not sure what we're going to pick up out of there. But it did confirm the boys' story.

'We found alcohol, found sick from where one of the boys had vomited. We believe the body was up in a corner, and we've been trying to take samples from up there. The odd bit of scraped flesh has been found, which we believe will be from the body. Everything so far corroborates what the teenagers have said.'

'Any hint they may be involved in this?'

'No,' said Ross. 'Parents are as frightened as anything. Angry at them. Ludlow's got no links to the kids at all. Also, if they did it, why would they turn around and tell us? And their story checks out so far. They stole the boat. Confirmed that with the owner. So far, everything they've said to us is true.'

'Okay, keep an eye on them, Ross. At the moment, they're witnesses, not to his death, but to certainly finding him.'

'I've sent a copy of my report over to you, Alan,' said Jona. She wouldn't call him Ross. She was forensics, not a direct member of the team. Jona dealt with everybody on first name terms, except for Perry; Perry felt like a first name.

'What'd you find?' asked Macleod, indicating Jona directly and not her team.

'Stephen Ludlow was stabbed with a serrated blade through the back. Whoever did this knew what they were doing. It wouldn't have taken long for him to die. Swift, from behind, at speed.'

'It's a surprise attack,' said Macleod.

'Surprise or quick? They might have been in front of him and spun round behind him. The precision of the blade, where it's gone, possibly military trained. It's that sort of level.'

'Okay,' said Macleod. 'So, what connection has he got to the military? Has he got any connection? Something to bear in mind.'

'I can't tell you if he was dead when he entered the cave or not. There's no clothing found. And he was naked,' said Jona. 'Can't find any blood in the cave.'

'So he'd stopped bleeding by that point. The wound—'

'Or it's washed away,' said Jona. 'He hadn't been there that long.'

'How long are we talking?' asked Macleod.

'Twenty-four hours before the boys found him, at most. It's hard to tell, the water doesn't help. But I would say he was dead twenty-four hours tops. That's your window before the boys got there.'

'So, the boys could have been seen?' pondered Macleod.

'One of the boys,' said Ross, 'speaking to me afterwards, known as Cheeks. Cheeks had found this cave previously, weeks and weeks ago. He'd planned to use it to bring a girl for the night. But for some reason, she didn't find it an attractive place to go for that sort of thing. So, he said, he took the lads instead for a bit of a piss-up.'

'So whoever placed the body there, they've obviously not been scoping the cave for a while. They would have seen him around there.'

'That's what I'm thinking,' said Ross.

'If you stash a body in a cave like that, how do you get it in?' asked Macleod.

'You could tether to it and swim it in,' said Jona. 'It's not that easy to get the boat in. The boys had a tiny boat. If you've got a body with you, you won't row it out like they did. You want it to be a lot quicker. You'd need a RIB, possibly.'

'How close to the cave can you get?' asked Macleod.

'If you're going to launch a boat to get there, come from the bay round the corner or the bay on the other side. So, the boys' rowboat took twenty minutes plus. I think unless you've got a motored boat, that's what you're going to take. If you've got a motorboat, you're going to make a lot of noise,' said Jona.

'Are there any other options?' asked Macleod.

'You could carry the body down there close to the cliff and get down the rocks with it,' said Jona. 'From what I saw, I can't find any evidence of that. You're not going to leave a lot behind if you do that. You could jump into the water with it. An excellent swimmer could swim the body inside. If there's more than one of you, of course, you could get in easily, lift it up, stash it in the cave and swim back out. Nobody would be none the wiser.'

'Why not leave it in the sea?' said Macleod.

'Because bodies in the sea come back to the surface,' said Jona. 'He'd turn up at some point.'

'And if he's just a missing man, we'd put out a search,' said Ross.

'He's disappeared. Who knows why?' said Jona. 'No body. No murder investigation. Who can find him?'

'Would anybody use the caves around there much?' asked Macleod.

Ross shook his head on the screen. 'Have you seen this place?

Have you seen how cold it is? There's no way you'd go near there. You don't swim in there by choice. And you're not going to go for a paddle off those rocks. There're bays either side, and they're a good bit away.'

'Really, they've been caught out because, well, teenage boys, isn't it?' said Macleod.

'Nutters,' said Ross. 'Absolute head cases going in there with booze and a boat. I mean, it's totally—'

'That's the thing about boys, isn't it?' said Macleod. 'They just do stuff, crazy stuff, won't look back.' He sat for a moment, thinking, lifting his coffee up and sipping it.

'Could Ludlow have gone in himself?'

'Well, he was a swimmer, champion swimmer,' said Ross, 'so he could have swum in—'

'There was no wetsuit. He wouldn't have swum in naked.'

'A champion swimmer,' said Ross, 'so he could have swum in naked.'

'Says you,' blurted Jona. 'You would not go into that water naked. Even these wild swimmers, they don't run in naked, you know. Water's cold, very cold. Even a champion swimmer wouldn't trust themselves.'

'Could he have met someone in there?' asked Macleod.

'He could have,' said Jona.

'And could they have stabbed him in there?'

'Well, there's a possibility. But to be honest, very convoluted. You both swim in there? Did you both go in there with a desire to do what? A meeting? A—'

'Well, thinking how our enterprising Mr Cheeks was thinking,' said Macleod. 'Maybe a rendezvous. Maybe there's a more adventurous woman that wanted our man.'

'Our man?' said Ross. 'We've no knowledge of his preferences or habits yet.'

'True,' said Macleod. 'Thank you, Ross. You're right.' He sipped more coffee, and there was a silence in the meeting for a moment. 'We haven't got a lot to go on at the moment. We need to find out where he's been, what he's done.'

'And I need you up here,' said Ross. 'Press are coming. It's not an easy place to control them. They're going to be everywhere. There's going to be speculation. There's going to be—'

'And you need to get on with investigating this. I get it, Ross,' said Macleod. 'I'll be up shortly. Got one or two things I have to tie up here, and then I'll make my way up.'

'I want to get back up too,' said Jona. 'Not much else I'm going to tell you from here. Reports will come in from our examinations. I'll keep you advised.'

'Good,' said Macleod. 'We'll see you later, Alan.'

'Yes sir. Bye, Jona,' said Ross.

Macleod gave a nod to Jona, and she looked at him for a moment, wondering what he wanted. Then she made her way over to his computer and closed down the call from their end. She then returned to the table.

'You're not calling Hope in?'

'She needs to be off. Do you know where she's gone at the moment?'

'Well, she was quiet. A little blip, I heard.'

'I can't say any more,' said Macleod. 'She's okay, though. They're just checking some things. I'm not dumping this on her because she'll come. She needs to look after herself at the moment.'

'Is that not her call?' said Jona.

'No, it's not,' said Macleod. 'I'm her boss, her employer. At the moment, she needs to look after herself. So, she needs that time, and she's getting it. Besides, I've done this sort of thing before,' he said, smiling.

'How are you finding it?' Jona said to him suddenly.

'What do you mean?'

'Soras, I've spent much time with you. Meditated with you, sat in sessions to get you back on your feet. I know you as well as most people here. In fact, I know you better than most people. There's maybe only Hope and Jane that know you any better than me. How are you finding not being at the coalface?'

'I'm getting more time with Jane,' said Macleod. 'Which is good. It's good for us. I'm not missing it.'

'Now you're lying,' she said.

'I am missing it. But I'm trying to do other things and taking on a wider scope. I'm now looking after an arts section. Developing up Clarissa, which, trust me, takes a bit of effort. I'm letting Hope run with it and I'm about to set up a new section. Plenty enough to do. I'm not just doing salaries and timesheets and things like that, not just covering off the press. Still in the thick of things, but I'm changing some stuff. I'm doing good.'

'But?' said Jona.

'But I'm missing it. It's me, it's what I'm built for.'

'And Hope really needs this time off? You're not just—'

'Hope needs this time,' said Macleod. 'And am I happy that she's not here to take it and that I can jump in and run with it? Oh yes,' he said. 'Absolutely. Do you know, Jane said to me, "You can stop packing that bag and leaving it in the car." The one in case we get called off somewhere. The one with a couple of days' clothing in it. I never not have it with me. That's how much I miss it.' He smiled.

'Oh well,' said Jona. 'You'll enjoy this one then.'

'Enjoy?' said Macleod. 'Somebody's dead.'

'Yes,' said Jona. 'I have that too. I enjoy my work. Bit gruesome though. Thanks for the coffee.'

She drained her mug, put it down, and then left the room. Macleod tidied the cups together, took them outside to the kitchen, where he washed them himself. He then came back and looked at the map on his wall.

Right at the top. He'd been there before, of course—many's a time in his life. In terms of cases, the last one he'd been to up there, someone had been eaten through the stomach by a rat. That was not a good time. But he had to admit, he missed times like that.

Chapter 04

Ross got off the call to Macleod and Jona to find Perry awaiting him outside the room. Although the man looked as slovenly as ever, there was a half-smile across his face.

'Have you come across something?' asked Ross.

'I've found Ludlow's girlfriend. Tabitha Green. She's staying in a hotel in Thurso. I thought you'd want to come to talk to her as well.'

'Absolutely,' said Ross. 'You can drive over.'

Perry nodded, and the two men walked in silence down to the car. Once they got in and begun to drive, Perry put on the radio, but at a low level, while Ross stared out.

'What do you know about her?' Ross asked Perry.

'She's staying in Thurso. She hadn't called in because she didn't think there was anything wrong with him missing. Having completed informing his family, that is his parents, we found out she was his girlfriend. One of the uniforms went round to inform her.'

'And she's up staying in Thurso? That's just along from here.'

'Apparently that's not where Stephen Ludlow was staying— at least, not these last lot of days. Anyways, I'm sure she'll be able to explain it when we get there.'

'Seems a little unusual, doesn't it?' queried Ross.

'Yes,' said Perry, 'it does. It seems unusual. If your girlfriend was up, you'd want her to be with you, wouldn't you? What would be the problem?'

'She might shed some light on what he was doing, though,' said Ross.

'We'll soon find out,' said Perry.

He turned the radio up a little louder as the two of them drove across in the afternoon sunshine. Ross could see the enormous clouds, however, rolling across the sky. Underneath them would be hail, maybe a bit of snow. But as long as they stayed away, the day was glorious, if cold.

Ross found the top end of the north of Scotland to be a bit strange as he drove. So very flat compared to around Inverness. That was because he was constantly driving along the coast. If he came up the east side, it certainly wasn't as flat. And he felt a touch off, as if he wasn't really on home turf. Of course, the unit covered here as much as anywhere else.

But they hadn't been up here that often. Not since, well, not since the one they all remembered. That one. The one with the rats. The one with the man and his medieval torturing of people.

There was a large chain hotel on the edge of Thurso that Tabitha Green was staying in. Budget-friendly, while still comfortable. And as people always said about it, at least, you knew what you were getting. As Ross and Perry pulled up, they were met by a constable who showed them up to a room on the third floor. Inside, sitting on a sofa beside a large double bed, was a blonde-haired woman.

Her hair rolled down to her shoulders, and she had a pleasant face. She was dressed in a green T-shirt and blue jeans. While not having a curvaceous figure, it was certainly well-toned.

'My name's Detective Sergeant Alan Ross. This is Detective Constable Warren Perry,' said Ross on arrival. 'I'm very sorry for your loss.'

The woman didn't say anything, tears in her eyes, but she sniffed occasionally.

'We're looking for a little more information,' said Ross, 'about what Stephen was doing in the area. I was wondering if you could help with that. Obviously, you've, what, come up together?'

'That was a while ago. Four or five days,' said the woman.

'Well, if you can help us, Miss Green, that would be much appreciated.'

'Tabby,' said the woman. 'I go by Tabby. I'm Tabitha Green, but I go by Tabby.' She looked like she was struggling and took a deep breath before continuing.

'Stephen was up here to set up links with some wild swimming clubs. They were looking to become part of his franchise. He's had massive success recently. So we were going to come up, and he was going to do that business. We'd have a couple of days after, and then we were off to London because Stephen was getting a knighthood.'

'And you didn't stay together while here?'

'Well, Stephen was going west along the coast. He picked out a few places to stop in. B&Bs and that. Or at least that's what he said he'd done. I don't know where he had booked.'

'Who normally books everything for him?' asked Ross.

'He has a secretary back in the office. She would do a lot of the trips, but Stephen was prone to just deciding to do things on his own. He liked to do things on the hoof sometimes. That

33

could be awkward. I like somewhere that I know what I'm getting and know what's happening. That's why I'm in here.'

'Do you know who he was visiting, though?'

'Well, there was Strathy Beach; he was going to Fresgoe as well, and Melvich. He said they had websites, because he had looked them up when he knew he was meeting them.'

'Can you explain to me a bit about how the franchise thing works?' asked Ross.

'Well, Stephen's got a name, and he's got a major website. He takes a cut off the top. People don't pay an exorbitant amount, but they join the club, and they maybe pay a pound each time they go to swim. There's always stuff put on for them, and they can record what they did. Some of them actually do swimming. There's a lot of merchandise they can buy which supports it as well, and it's worked really, really well. Stephen was a champion open water swimmer, but there's not a lot of money in that.

'This was his way of channelling what he did to make money for the future. He's . . . well, despite being a champion—he's still a strong swimmer—but to compete at that level, once you get into your forties, you're, well, on the way down, I guess.'

Ross looked over and saw Perry nodding, although Ross wasn't sure that Perry was particularly of that level when he was younger, anyway.

'So when he goes to visit these franchises, what does he do? How does it work? Have you ever been with him on any?' asked Ross.

'Yes, I've been to a few, not many. He joins them. They go for a swim where they would normally take people for their open water swimming. He assesses it, he looks at their facilities, tells them what they have to do to get up to speed. If it's all going well, he shows them the contracts over dinner. They look into it. There're certain safeguards and insurance and that has to go with it as well. Hell, Stephen takes care of a lot over that.'

'And you say it's gone really well?'

'Last three years from a tiny start, it's grown well. The first year, he made just about enough to cover himself for living. Last year, much more. This year, really, it's turned into a proper business.'

'How much of a proper business?' asked Ross.

'He's going to turn over a million.'

'And profit from that?' asked Ross.

'Hundreds of thousands, at least. I don't actually know the numbers.'

'Forgive me for being indelicate,' said Perry. 'If I could just ask, who runs it now? Who gets the benefit of it?'

Tabby looked over at him sharply. 'It's not me, if that's what you're implying.'

'DC Perry was not implying anything,' said Ross. 'It's a reasonable question to ask. I suspected it might not be you, as you're not a spouse. But do you know who would benefit from it?'

'His family, I guess,' said Tabitha. 'I guess probably his mother and father.'

Ross nodded, sat back for a moment, but Perry leaned forward. 'If you have a list of these clubs, addresses and that— I know you've given us the names—that would be helpful, Tabitha.'

She stood up, went across to the desk, and started flicking through a folder. She turned round and almost threw it at Perry.

'They're all in there. The schedule, everything. Where he was trying to go. The names of the people too.'

'Did he not have it with him?' asked Perry.

'We both have copies. Contacts in case I need to get hold of him.'

'Does he have a mobile?' asked Perry.

'Trying to get Stephen on his mobile, it's like trying to resurrect Lord Lucan. Never know if he'll answer, when he'll answer. He closed down calls sometimes when I tried to contact him.'

'If you don't mind me asking,' said Perry, 'can I ask a little about your relationship? When you met, how you met?'

'I'm an open water swimmer,' said Tabby.

Ross looked at her. She certainly had a figure, but didn't look like a model. She looked like a strong woman. A sportswoman. She wasn't unattractive. Far from it. But she was definitely on the muscly side. In fact, Ross believed her arms had more muscles than his. Although, as he regretted, it probably wasn't that difficult.

'I met him at a competition. And, well, we got close and pretty soon we were together.'

'Have you anything beyond the open water swimming that you do together?' asked Perry.

'It consumes his life. It's what he likes to do. Go out in the open. I'm not so keen at this time of year. In the summer, yes. I wouldn't be for roaming around too often, just do the swim, but he would sit and eat and drink on the beach in this weather. It's Baltic. I'm afraid I would head south, France somewhere, further south, Spain, anywhere warm,' said Tabby.

'So what sort of person was he?' asked Ross.

'Consumed by his open water swimming; the business took

the rest of him.'

'You feel left behind?' asked Perry. The woman flinched. *He must have hit the nail on the head,* thought Ross.

'At times. But it's business, isn't it? He has to get it going. It'll be the rest of our livelihood, or it would have been. I'm not sure I could take it on. The parents wanted me to be in the company with him,' said Tabby. 'Haven't got the name. He had the name. Publicity was coming in. It was all good. Really, really good.'

'Had he ever had any problems?' asked Perry.

'Not really. Well . . .'

'What?' asked Ross.

'We had a girl working for us. She accused him—well, she didn't accuse him. She said that he took her away.'

'And what?' asked Perry.

'Had sex with her.'

'She was what age?' probed Perry.

'Sixteen,' said Tabby. 'I think she was lying, though. The papers did not catch on like she hoped. The newspapers didn't receive her favourably either. A lot of holes in her story. It was blown out of the water quickly. Set us back a few months, though. We had to make sure that we weren't going to invest a lot of money and then get hit by that.'

'And you think he didn't?'

'Stephen's lovely. He's beautiful. Sorry, he was. I can understand how especially a young lass could fall for him. He might have seemed like he liked the ladies, but he was just good at bringing people in, and a good-looking man with women, sometimes that's how you play it. You're a dreamboat, aren't you? You don't actually fulfil any fantasies. Just be that person who they like to think about. But he was faithful to me.'

'What's your plans?' asked Ross.

'I don't know. Guess I should see Stephen's family at some point.'

'Where are they?' asked Ross.

'Back down in Suffolk. But I can't face them at the moment.'

'If you're going to leave the area, can you tell me?'

'Of course,' said Tabby.

Ross handed over a card. 'I just need you to be contactable given the circumstances.'

'I understand,' she said. Ross stood up and thanked the woman, passing his condolences again, with Perry following in his wake as he left the room. As they got downstairs to the car, Ross looked across at Perry.

'Hope always says you know your stuff regarding people. What do you make of her?'

'Jealous,' said Perry. 'Especially that sixteen-year-old. And who can blame her? I mean, she's right. Hot Stephen Ludlow. I know he was dead when we saw him but he obviously had looks. And so does she,' said Perry. 'Very fit, very trim.

'Imagine a woman of that age gets undercut by a sixteen-year-old. You're not going to be happy, are you? Also, going to question yourself. I wonder how that went. I wonder what really went on between the two of them.'

'Well, you're only going to hear one side of the story,' said Ross.

'I'm not so sure about her,' said Perry. 'It's funny, isn't it? She stays in a hotel while he goes off and sees these other people and then stays where? A B&B somewhere? Why? Why wouldn't he come back to her? I mean, what else was pulling him away from coming back to her? It's not even that long a taxi ride along here. If you're making the sort of money she was talking about, stick it on the business. It's not a problem.'

'You definitely have something there,' said Ross. 'Let's make a call to Thurso Police Station. I want to set up properly in there. The boss will be up soon, and if we can do that before tonight, when he's here, we can get out and see these groups. It'll be important to get a hold of them quickly.'

'It seems an awful kerfuffle,' said Perry. 'Stick him in the cave. You don't want his body to turn up. Why is it so important that he doesn't turn up? You know?'

'Maybe you want to leave the area. Be well clear beforehand.'

'That's true,' said Perry, 'but look around us. Look at the area. Get a spade. Go into one of these fields and dig deep. Somewhere near some trees. Bury him there. Who in their right mind is going to be looking to dig him up?'

'You don't get any dog walkers inside a sea cave.'

'I suppose so,' said Perry. 'Still seems a bit much to me.'

'Maybe it's their forte. If you're a strong swimmer, you could get out there. Maybe they're thinking not many people will find it. Unlucky with the boys finding it. If you don't have kids, you might think like that,' said Ross.

'Does it not bother you, though?' said Perry.

'Bother me? What do you mean?' said Ross.

'When your little one grows up, he's going to be a boy like this lot. Start racing off for a night of booze or, even worse, take a young lady out to places like these.'

'I think I've got enough to worry about at the moment before thinking about that.'

'You're probably not wrong there,' said Perry.

He went to the driver's seat and Ross got in beside him. But this was a time of investigation he didn't like. Ross liked lines to follow, leads to chase down, liked when things were becoming more apparent. He wanted to get behind his computer and dig things up about people. He was out in front here and, in truth, he wasn't feeling that happy about it.

Chapter 05

The front desk of the Thurso Police Station was not the busiest in the country. The older man attending to it heard a rap on the frosted glass and slid back the window to see a man standing there in a long, dark coat with a fedora hat on top. He had a scarf wrapped around his neck and gave a smile.

'Where's the best place to park?' he said.

'There're some areas in town, a few car parks there. They're probably safe enough. If you head back down that way—'

'No,' said the man, 'here at the station.'

'That's only for officers and staff attached to the station.'

The man before him reached inside under his coat, and pulled out a warrant card that said 'Detective Chief Inspector, Seoras Macleod.' The man behind the desk wanted to crawl away somewhere and hide.

'My apologies, Chief Inspector, I don't think we've ever met.'

'Well, I hope not,' said Macleod. He gave a bit of a smile, while the other man continued to try to retract further behind the opening.

'The car?'

'I'll park it for you,' said the man suddenly.

'But that means you would have to leave here,' said Macleod. 'I might be a chief inspector, but I'm actually still fit enough to park my car. So, if you just tell me where the car park is—'

'Down the road, swing round the back, and take any space in there, Chief Inspector.'

'Seoras,' he said. It would have been correct for the man to have given his own first name back, but the way the word 'Seoras' was termed, it didn't sound like that was going to happen.

'Yes, Chief Inspector. Chief Inspector Seoras Macleod. I'll remember that, sir.'

Macleod turned away with a grin and several minutes later had parked the car and entered through the rear of the police station. It wasn't large, but when he stepped inside, Alan Ross met him.

'You're here, sir.'

'Yes, indeed I am,' said Macleod.

'This way through. I think they've got coffee ready.'

'You realise, Ross, that I actually don't judge what's going on by whether coffee has turned up?'

Ross gave him a look. Macleod thought he was questioning him with that stare.

'How are we getting on?'

'Well,' Ross said, 'I think we're about to go out and interview people. I wondered if you would want to take one of the interviews.'

'Into the room and we'll talk about it,' said Macleod.

Ross led him into a compact room with a table and chairs. Perry was sitting there, one leg up across his knee, as was Susan Cunningham in her jeans, t-shirt, and long blonde ponytail. She gave a smile as Macleod walked in.

'Everything good?' Macleod asked her.

'Fine. Legs holding up well.'

'Perry, all good?'

Perry gave a shake of his shoulders. Macleod understood that wasn't a complaint. What it meant was that Perry wasn't on top of the case yet and didn't have a full understanding. If he did, Macleod would race off to find the suspect that Perry wanted. The man was good, very good. But what he didn't really have was Hope at the moment.

Hope was different, by the book, thorough. She complimented Macleod well. Instead, he had Alan Ross. Ross was always the good third party for Macleod. He did a lot of the spade work, ran around and did everything for him. But he was number two here. He couldn't have him do that. He'd have to issue that out to Perry or Susan. Macleod would need to make sure that he told Ross that. Or at least that Ross did it.

'So what's the deal?' asked Macleod.

'Stephen Ludlow had a girlfriend staying here in Thurso. She's still in the hotel at the moment. Her name's Tabitha Green, known as Tabby. An open water swimmer herself. And she's twenty-five.'

'Blonde, good looking. Can see why he was with her,' said Perry.

'I think we can phrase it better than that,' said Ross.

'Would Stephen Ludlow phrase it different to that, though?' said Macleod. 'That's the real question. Go on, Ross.'

'She says they were up here looking at potential franchises and franchisees. She reckons Stephen was out swimming with them. He'd be understanding their operation, dining with them, and then looking at signing contracts. That's where he's been for the last couple of days. She hasn't had contact with him.'

'No contact?' said Macleod. 'That's unusual, isn't it?'

'She says not so,' said Ross.

'Not close then.'

'Not in each other's pockets anyway,' said Susan Cunningham.

'So what's the plan, Ross?' asked Macleod.

'I think we talk to these franchisees. See what he was saying and what he did with them. See if we can spot anything unusual. Otherwise, if it's not something from up here, it's going to be further afield. We'll be looking for someone in his immediate past, or further back. There's a potential young woman. But if we start here and then look further back in his past, it would be a better idea with our resources,' said Ross.

'Very good,' said Macleod. 'That sounds like a plan to me. Where are we going?'

'We've got Strathy Beach for the Achterbergs,' said Ross. 'We've got Fresgoe Bathers, a Gail Horman, and we've got a foreign group of ladies down at Melvich. Also, Jona is coming up here later tonight.'

'Okay,' said Macleod. 'Why don't I go to Strathy with Susan? Ross, you and Perry go to Fresgoe, and then Melvich. Both tonight. I want to talk later on about what's going on with those people. I'll have seen Jona by that point, to see if she's got anything further. Also, keep looking out for other things around them, okay? At the moment, these aren't suspects, but they're people of interest. I want to know everything about them,' said Macleod.

See if there're any links. Ross is right. We cover off the local area, and then we spread it back out, because maybe it isn't anything to do with people up here. Maybe it's somebody who followed him up here. Maybe putting him stashed away in a cave is their time to get away. If he's then found months, weeks later, a much colder trail. Anyway, let's get cracking.'

Perry stood up, but noticed Macleod didn't move.

'I meant after the coffee,' said Macleod.

Susan laughed. Perry gave a shake of his head. 'I'm not sure you're going to get the good stuff up here, I don't know if—'

'Ross always finds the good stuff, Perry. If you're on coffee duty, you better make sure you come up to speed,' said Macleod.

Susan laughed again and drunk her own. Ten minutes later, Susan Cunningham and Macleod were driving out to Strathy Bay Bathers. Susan had phoned ahead, having found the owners on a website.

'We're going to speak to Alec and Wendy Achterberg.'

'Achterberg,' said Macleod. 'German? Austrian?'

'That area,' she said. 'I think, possibly Dutch. I don't know.'

'Well, we'd better find out.'

Even though it was dark as they pulled up, Macleod could see a glorious house sitting not far off the roadside overlooking Strathy Beach. The beach was a beautiful run of sand, but in the darkness, little could be seen of it. However, the house was lit up around the outside with spotlights here and there showcasing its beauty.

There was a large barn area at the rear, and the place certainly seemed to be something that Macleod would struggle to afford. It was a beautiful place. His own house on the Black Isle hadn't been cheap, but it wasn't like this.

Susan pulled the car up at the top end of the drive, and together they approached the front door. The doorbell made a rather long, chiming noise, causing Macleod to raise his eyebrows. But when the door opened, they were greeted by a woman, probably close to Macleod's age. She had brown hair, not quite dark, but certainly not light, and wore a white blouse with a rather demure brown skirt beneath it. Her face showed the lines of age, but for all that, it was attractive. She had thick eyebrows and a gentle smile.

'My name's Wendy Achterberg,' she said as she opened the door. 'You must be . . .'

'Detective Chief Inspector Seoras Macleod,' said Macleod, pulling out his warrant card. 'This is Detective Constable Susan Cunningham.'

'Well, come in, come in. Terrible business,' said Wendy.

She guided Macleod through to a rather glamorous living room and deposited him on a large sofa. Susan sat at the other end of the sofa, leaning forward with her notepad out as a man walked into the room.

He had grey hair either side of a receded black patch at the top. He was certainly Macleod's age. But he was broad and had a rather military bearing. A large nose with a chiselled chin showed someone who was keeping in shape, despite his years. He wore a green shirt with green trousers and reminded Macleod of either a park ranger or a military officer who was no longer on duty.

'Good evening, sir. Detective Inspector Seoras Macleod. This is Detective Constable Susan Cunningham.'

'Alec Achterberg. I'd like to say it's a pleasure to meet you, Inspector, but given the circumstances . . .'

'No, quite,' said Macleod. 'Thank you for seeing us on such short notice. We're here, obviously, to ask about Stephen Ludlow, so if you could just tell us about meeting him this week, where and when. How you made contact with him, your dealings with him regarding the possible franchise of your wild swimming contingent.'

'But of course,' said Alec. 'To be honest, he came here, what was it, two days ago, three—three days ago? Yes, it was three, wasn't it, Wendy?'

Wendy nodded. 'Delightful man. Just coming over his prime, I would say. Certainly very fit. Very with it.'

'Wendy took quite a liking to him, didn't you?' said Alec.

'The sort of man you'd want for a son. Quick with it, talked well, but very polite. Excellent swimmer, too,' said Wendy.

'So how did the day pan out for you?' asked Susan.

'Well, he came up here about, what, half nine. We were in the water by half ten. He'd never been out on the beach down here at Strathy. He enjoyed that, and then he went for lunch with us. We talked a bit in the afternoon, and then we went for dinner. Rather posh place, in fact.'

'Just the three of you?'

'I actually had a bit of business,' said Alec. 'It was just Wendy for about an hour or two. But he seemed quite engaged with Wendy, didn't he?'

'Very much,' said Wendy. 'I guess he was a charming man. Charming. Such a pity. I enjoyed . . .' she broke up for a moment. 'I enjoyed meeting him. I don't know what it means for the franchise, either.'

'Were you going to go with it?' asked Macleod. 'Join him?'

'Oh, absolutely,' said Alec. 'We're not that long up here. And this has been one thing that's certainly worked well for us. Started to get to know people. But we've also been joined every now and again by tourists coming through. You join these franchises, people will then come through the summer. Maybe more. I think we could turn it into much more than a swim with the business. Not just the swim, but other things around it. We might open a small cafe or . . . We'll see. We'll see what we're going to do. Of course, not sure how that all works now.'

'And Stephen was enthusiastic too about it?' asked Susan.

'Buzzing. Absolutely buzzing,' said Wendy. 'He dealt with all our issues. We were talking about insurance, about who can be part of the group. My lack of experience of dealing with people. Alec, of course, has a military background. He's talked to people before. Not a problem.'

'What military background is that?' asked Macleod.

'I was with the South African Army for a while.'

'Achterberg, what is that? Where's it from?' asked Macleod.

'It's a Dutch name. I was born in Holland. Sorry, in the Netherlands. But then I was moved with the family to South Africa. In the South African Army for several years. I've come back to retire. Well, Wendy's from here, you see. This is Wendy's area.'

'When were you in the South African Army?'

'Well, I quit thirty years ago. So actually, I've been in Britain for quite a while.'

'And you did what?' asked Macleod.

'Well, I kicked about down south for a bit, tried to get some various businesses going. Then I met Wendy and, well, I recently moved up here.'

'Why was that?' asked Susan.

'New start, great place to be away from people. Wendy loves it too.'

'I wasn't keen at the start,' said Wendy, 'but now I've come here, yes, it's been a good choice. Alec certainly knew what he was talking about. I'm looking forward to the business. I hope it doesn't end with this. Is there any reason we should be worried?'

'I don't see why,' said Macleod. 'I am talking to you because you're some of the last people to have seen him, that's all.'

'Did he say where he was staying, by the way?' asked Susan.

'No,' said Alec. 'Not a word about that. He didn't drink all night so when he left us he was in his own car.'

'What car was that?' asked Susan.

Alec stopped to think. 'Hire car, I think. Black. Small and black. I don't know beyond that.'

'Okay,' said Macleod. 'If you think of anything else to tell us about him, please do. You can contact me here on this number.' He handed a card over to Alec. 'We may come back for further questions. We're tracing his last days, what happened, so there may be other questions to come back with depending on other inquiries. Thank you for your candour so far,' said Macleod, 'and we'll be in touch if necessary.'

They stepped outside, back into the car and as Susan drove down the driveway, Macleod said to her, 'Obviously been successful in the past. That's quite a house. Seems strange to suddenly come up here and run a wild swimming franchise. I think we need to investigate his background a bit more.'

'Military background. What did Jona say about the serrated blade? Somebody who would know how to kill.'

'Well, that ties up,' said Macleod. 'But well, you still have to have a reason.'

'Maybe he said no to giving them a franchise,' said Susan.

'So what, they just killed him? It's a harsh reaction. And if you're going to do that, why not do it once they've left here? Otherwise, you make yourself a suspect. Susan,' said Macleod. 'I think there's a bit more digging to do.'

Chapter 06

Ross and Perry headed for Fresgoe, a small village along the north coast. A Gail Harman ran a small social group of swimmers there called Fresgoe Swimmers, and Perry had contacted her in her small flat. She said she would be in for the evening and they were to just drop in.

When they got there, Perry saw the flat was a house that had been divided into four. Not uncommon in Scotland and something that had seen a greater abundance for single folk in options of housing. As he walked up to the door, Perry knocked on it with his hand, realising there was no rapper. A young woman came down the stairs and opened the door, staring at the two men.

She hid in the shadow, not wanting to step out to see them, and asked politely who they were.

'I'm Detective Sergeant Alan Ross,' said Ross, displaying his warrant card. 'This is Detective Constable Warren Perry, who spoke to you earlier on the phone. Are you Miss Gail Harman?'

'Just Gail, thank you,' said the woman. 'Come in; come in.'

She moved further back into the shadow, pulling the door open, and Perry could see steps up towards a flat. However, there was no landing light on. As Ross stepped in, Gail apologised, reached across, and flicked the light switch, illuminating the stairs before them. They were carpeted in a peach colour and Perry was wondering whether his shoes were ill-advised for this type of carpet. However, Ross made his way up. Perry followed and Gail shut the door behind them.

The flat was intimate. Perry guessed there was one bedroom off to the side, for they didn't get taken through that door. He could see a small kitchenette and then the living room that they were taken into.

Gail sat on a reclining chair while Perry and Ross sat down on a small sofa. Perry looked uncomfortable, as if the chair didn't match his size, like an adult going into primary school and using their chairs. He felt slightly self-conscious, especially looking at Gail Harman.

Gail had light brown hair that swung down the side of her face. She was trim and had a beaming white smile. She certainly looked as if she was fit—toned and muscular. Perry thought there were far too many toned and muscular people around at the moment, and was feeling very self-conscious about it. However, she certainly looked the part. He'd seen Tabitha Green earlier on, and Gail was very much in the same mode.

'I have got little in,' said Gail suddenly. 'A cup of tea or coffee or that—'

'There's no need to be nervous,' said Ross. 'We're just here to ask a few questions. You probably heard about the untimely demise of Stephen Ludlow. You and several other potential franchise owners were the last people to see him, we believe, and so we're just tracing his movements. When did you see him?'

'Two days ago,' said Gail. 'He came and spent the day with

51

me.'

'This was for the franchise?' asked Ross.

'Yes, yes,' said Gail suddenly. 'It was for the franchise. He, well, he was rather charming, very—'

'Very what?' asked Perry.

'Pleasant,' said Gail suddenly. Perry thought she meant anything but pleasant. Not in the nasty sense, but in the glad-to-see-him sense.

'What exactly happened on the day?' asked Ross.

'He came here about nine in the morning. We chatted up here in my flat. We went down to the bay, for a swim. In fact, we swam for quite a while. Then he took me out to lunch. Then we talked back here in the afternoon. And then he took me to dinner.'

'And did he leave after dinner?' asked Ross, then wished he'd put that in a better fashion.

'Not directly,' said Gail. 'He came up here for a while. We had some coffee. We were discussing the franchise.'

'And how did those discussions go?' asked Perry.

'He was very keen. We were both very keen. I'm, well, I'm not the most social of people.'

'Why's that?' asked Perry.

Gail looked across. There was a photo of a man on her mantelpiece. He was young, possibly a touch younger than Gail currently.

'That's my husband. Or was my husband. That's Carl.'

'Was your husband?' said Perry. 'What happened?'

'I was a competitive swimmer, competitive wild swimmer. That's where I met Carl. We were on the scene together in competitive outdoor swimming and, well, we got together and got married. I left the sport because he died during training.

He was out for a swim one day and they didn't find him. They found his tether, then didn't find him. Gone to the sea—never came back alive.'

'I'm so sorry,' said Perry. 'That must have been devastating.'

'It is; it was. Anyway, I moved. Been up here now for, oh, what, five years?'

'What age were you when he passed, then?' asked Ross.

'Twenty. Well, we were young. Had a short time together. Only had six months married. But they were some of the best times of my life. And then I lost him. It's taken me a while to get back. I came up here initially to just be away from people. Be away from all the drama. But I've got a small group that now swims with me. I'm trying to get back out.

'And I saw the franchise as a way to make money and do what I know how to do. I can swim well. I understand swimming and I understand other people swimming. How to help them too. That sort of thing, you know.'

'And so, Stephen was going to help you with that?'

'He understood all the other sides of it. The insurance and building people up. He was taking away a lot of the initial set-up problems. We had a lot in common. He was an ex-swimmer too. I used to know about him, knew his name. I'd actually seen him before, when I was very young, swimming in competitions. He was good. Really good. To be honest, I was star-struck with him coming up to see me.'

'And the day went well then?' asked Perry.

'Very well. Very well indeed.'

'Can I ask you,' said Perry, 'he came in a car? Was it his own?'

'Yes, it was his own, I think. I don't know. Could have been a hire car for all I know.' Gail stopped for a moment. 'It was black. It was small and black. Immaculate inside. It was certainly spotless.'

'And he left then, in the evening. Do you know where he went?'

Gail stopped for a moment.

'I guess I probably have to tell you this.'

'Tell us what?' asked Ross.

The woman stood up for a moment, walked over to the window. She looked out towards the sea. 'I'm not very proud of it.'

'Proud of what?' asked Ross for a moment, worried that things were about to take a very unsavoury turn.

'I asked him to stay. I asked him to stay the night.'

'And did he?' asked Ross.

'It gets lonely,' she said. 'Do you understand that? It gets lonely. And he was so lovely. Everything about him, his shape, his eyes, his hair, his way with me. We had so much to talk about. When we swam, it was like—' She sat down again, clutching her hands in towards her bosom.

'Did he stay over?' asked Perry.

'He did. But he left the next morning. Check with my neighbours. I'm sure they'll know. They're always watching. Especially—'

'Your neighbours are always watching?' asked Perry.

'Especially Mr Dawes. Mr Dawes is the worst. I don't like him at all. He said to me that morning, because I came down with Stephen. I wasn't intending to come out of the flat because I only had my gown on. I mean, it's not a rude gown or anything. You can't see anything. But I came down, and I walked with Stephen out to his car. Kissed him there. And he drove off. And I was coming back into the flat, and Mr Dawes made his way out from his door past me, and he just said, 'I bet you enjoyed him.'

'That's a bit rude,' said Ross.

'He's always rude. Not always sexually rude, just rude. Complains about everything, watches me and everything.'

'Do you know where Stephen went after this?' asked Perry.

'Well, that day, he was going down to see some other people. I think there's a couple of people who do what I want to do. But they do it further down at Melvich.'

'These places are all kind of close together,' said Perry. 'Are you worried that he wouldn't have given the franchise to you?'

'That's not why I slept with him,' said Gail.

'I wasn't suggesting that,' said Perry, 'but with so many franchises that close, are there enough people? Is there room for three businesses?'

'I don't know what he said to any of the rest of them, but he was very keen to have me on board.'

Gail stood up again, out to the window and looked out to the sea. 'They say they found him out there. The lifeboat found him.'

'That's true,' said Perry. 'Do you go swimming much out of the bay when you wild swim?'

'No! You don't do that,' said Gail. 'That would be a bad idea. Up round here, further out, you don't know what you're getting into. I've swum round here for several years. I strictly keep my bathers in close. Most of them aren't swimmers. Most of them are bathing. They come in, they get immersed, and they get back out. There's one or two who swim, but they're not that strong. I wouldn't let them swim any further out. I don't like to swim much further out, and I know what I'm doing,' said Gail, defensively.

'Clearly, you've been lonely. Has the group helped you?'

asked Perry.

'This group has got me back out, talking to people, doing things. It's now brought me a man I went to bed with. That was a step, too. Can you understand that? People like Mr Dawes don't understand that. They just see you having a quiet brief fling on the side, but I mean, Stephen doesn't have anyone. I didn't—nothing wrong with it.'

'Did he ever mention the name Tabitha Green to you, or Tabby?' asked Perry.

'Yes, she helps them with the business. He said I would see her name on certain bits and pieces, or she might answer the phone.'

'I'm afraid that's his girlfriend.'

Gail put her hand up to her chest again, almost as if she was about to hyperventilate.

'He never said. If I knew he was with someone, I wouldn't have . . .'

'I'm sure you wouldn't have,' said Ross. 'And neither of us are accusing you. Constable Perry's just informing you of a rather unfortunate fact.'

'Oh, dear God,' said Gail. 'That poor girl. And to think that I . . .'

'It's okay,' said Perry. 'Can I just ask one thing? Your husband died while out swimming. Was there an inquest?'

'Yes, yes,' said Gail, almost relieved to move on to a different subject, despite how hard this subject should have hit her as well. 'He died of . . . unexplained causes. They don't know what happened to him. His float should have stayed intact if he'd had a heart attack or something.

'He was a strong swimmer. There was no reason. The tides didn't look bad. But his float wasn't attached to him. It had come away. He never surfaced for three days. Then he was washed ashore. There was nothing on him. No mark. Nothing to say what had happened to him. Except that he'd drowned. His lungs were full of water.'

'Thank you,' said Perry. 'That must have been hard to talk about.'

'Are you going anywhere?' asked Ross.

'No,' Gail said.

'If you do, contact me,' said Ross, handing over a card. 'Please do contact me. Don't talk to anyone else about you and Stephen being together for that night.'

'I won't,' said Gail. 'Please don't tell his girlfriend unless you really have to. Oh, I feel dreadful. I feel so dreadful. Especially because I enjoyed it. I'd missed it so much. Do you know that? I—'

'We may be back to talk to you,' said Perry. 'In the meantime, take it easy. You've nothing to be ashamed of.'

'Thank you,' she said.

Together, Perry and Ross left the flat. When they got outside to the car, they could see a man looking out of his window towards them.

'Mr Dawes there? Maybe he'll think we've had sex with her, too,' said Perry.

Ross rolled his eyes at him. 'What do you make of her?'

'Genuine,' said Perry. 'Very genuine. Troubled soul. Obviously been messed up.'

'So, you think she's telling us the truth?'

'I think she's telling us her truth,' said Perry. 'What the actual truth of it all is, I don't know. Still to be found out. But we'll see. But I think she's telling us how she saw it all.'

'We best get on. We've got these two foreign women to talk

to now,' said Ross.

'Quite a good wee run for him, isn't it?' said Perry suddenly.

'What do you mean?' said Ross.

'No offence,' said Perry. 'You may not clock it the way I do. Gail there, good-looking woman, and very like Tabitha. Tabitha, she was well-toned, similar to Gail. That sort of fitness look of a woman. A woman who's trim, lean, not curvy, not that sort of model-type thing. Or rather, more like a catwalk model. Actually, no, not thin, muscly. Maybe that's what Stephen liked.'

'And you think the next two will be like that?'

'Wait and see,' said Perry. 'Maybe he played away too much. Maybe somebody didn't like it.'

'That's just one thing everybody says. Everybody tries to put everything down to sex. Not everyone's like that.'

'They're not,' said Perry. 'Trouble is, in too many of these cases, it is about that. It's about who's with who, who saw who, who thinks they're with who. Either that or money, and the odd case of religion. They say that, don't they? Drivers in life: money, sex, religion. Drives what everybody does.'

'Speak for yourself,' said Ross. 'Religion doesn't drive me. You?'

'To be honest, religion doesn't have the hold it used to,' said Perry. 'The other two, probably still as strong.'

Chapter 07

T he headlights of the car cut through the darkness as Ross and Perry continued their journey further west to Melvich. Macleod had concluded his investigation at the Achterbergs and was off to meet up with Jona again. Meanwhile, Ross and Perry would interview Selina Soto and Carmen Cabral. Perry was wondering what sort of people they were, and also wondered just how Ross would take to them.

They sounded exotic. Whether they were was, of course, a different matter. But Perry was thinking they might be a little more colourful than Gail Harman. As the car pulled up to what looked like a fairly standard Scottish house for this part of the world—rather grey, drab exterior, box-like with a sloping roof—there were hints that the people who lived inside were a bit more exotic than that. On the driveway, lights had been put out, probably solar LEDs bought at a garden centre, marking the path to the front door.

Perry pulled on the handbrake. The air was nippy as they stepped out of the car and Ross pressed the doorbell. It gave a loud clacking sound. As the door opened, Perry had to take a second glance. Standing there was a dark-skinned woman with large frizzy hair, prominent lips, but a very trim figure. However, the reason that Perry had to take a second look was she was in a small pair of shorts and a half-cut T-shirt. Wasn't the woman aware of what time of year it was?

'Good evening,' said Ross. 'I'm Detective Sergeant Alan Ross. This is Detective Constable Warren Perry. We're here investigating the death of Stephen Ludlow, and we believe he saw you recently.'

'He's dead? How did that happen?'

Ross and Perry looked at each other in bewilderment.

'It's what all the commotion's been about with the lifeboat and the searching,' said Ross.

'Oh, right. Him, was it? Wow!'

'Are you Miss Soto?'

'I am. I'm Selina Soto,' said the woman, not really registering yet what Ross had said. 'And he's dead?'

'I'm afraid so. Mr Ludlow was found dead. We're trying to trace his last movements. We believe he came here for an interview with yourselves to talk about his franchise of wild swimming clubs.'

'That's correct. Carmen and I are going to set one up. Wow! Hang on a moment. Carmen, love,' she said. 'Carmen! It's the police.'

Behind Selina appeared a woman whose skin wasn't as dark, but which was still heavily tanned. She had frizzy hair worn up in a ponytail behind her, and she was wearing a dressing gown.

'Oh, hello,' she said.

She wrapped her arms around Selina, almost hugging into her, and rested her chin on her shoulder as she looked over at Perry. Perry saw that Selina never flinched. Normally, if a lover grabbed you from behind, or even just a close friend, there'd be some sort of appreciation of that hold, that tenderness. But Selina? She never flinched at all.

'Would it be possible to come in to talk?' said Ross. 'It's rather cold here on the doorstep.'

'Of course,' said Selina.

She turned, breaking away from Carmen, and the two women walked towards an interior door, leaving Ross to follow and Perry to close the front door after himself.

When Perry entered the living room, Selina had sat down on a single chair, while Carmen was on a sofa. Her bare legs were sticking out from underneath the dressing gown, which seemed to struggle to remain on her. Ross had sat down in the other single seat in the living room, leaving Perry to sit beside Carmen. It was a little awkward, and he'd rather that she went and got something more on, but he would not mention it. That would show he'd noticed.

'I'd like you to tell me about meeting Stephen Ludlow, and a little about your potential operation up here,' said Ross.

'Well,' said Selina, 'we've moved up north recently. You know, to get the good life. To seek a better way of living. We've come here to Melvich and it's lovely. It's cooler than what I'm used to.'

'Where are you from?' asked Perry.

'We've been in Europe for a bit. And then we were down in England,' said Carmen.

'Where are you from originally, though?' asked Perry.

'Well, I'm Spanish,' said Carmen. 'Or at least there's Spanish running in my blood. I was actually born in the UK. Selina, however, is from Chile.'

'Wow,' said Perry. 'I have to be honest, I've never actually met anyone from Chile. It looks a beautiful country with the mountains.'

'I was closer to the coast when I grew up,' said Selina. 'But I've been away a long time.'

'So how did you meet?' asked Ross.

'Spotted Selina on my travels around Europe. We hit it off and we've travelled together since.'

'So friends then, or . . .?'

'Friends,' said Selina. But Perry noticed a look from Carmen.

'I came over to get a university degree in business,' said Selina. 'I got one in Europe. That's when I met Carmen, and we came over here.'

'I used to be a competitive swimmer,' said Carmen. 'But I gave that up to move into business and have a better life. Competitive swimming's not the joy everybody thinks it would be.'

'Most top-level sport isn't,' said Perry, and took a look from Ross to say, 'How would you know?'

'Are you finding the climate here to your liking?' asked Ross.

'It takes a bit of getting used to, but we have a warm house.'

Perry could attest to that. He was currently sitting in his suit jacket and sweating heavily. It must have been at least twenty-three or twenty-four degrees in the room. He stood up and took his jacket off, and part of him wanted to hand it to Carmen. She clearly needed more clothing on.

'So, you saw Mr Ludlow when?'

'That would have been . . . not yesterday. No, it would have been yesterday, wouldn't it?' asked Selina

'Yes—yesterday,' confirmed Carmen. 'Selina gets a bit absent-minded at times. It wasn't yesterday, it was the day before, Selina.'

'It was, of course,' Selina said, shaking her head.

'And what was the plan for the day?' asked Ross.

'He came over quite early,' said Carmen. 'I rarely get up that early, but at nine o'clock he arrived. By ten we were out in the bay, swimming with him. He was very thorough. Asked us about all the dangers of wild swimming, what we would do, what equipment we had; asked about numbers in the club. Well, we're not that big yet. There's about ten of us, but we're looking to do it more on a commercial level. And we were gauging his thoughts on that.'

'Are you aware there's several other groups here?'

'If you can call them that,' said Carmen. 'We're looking to do a much more professional club. Selina's got the business head for it, and I've got the water experience. I think people will probably find a better experience with us.'

'We'll know how to keep people safe. We'll know how to attract people there, and also attract tourists,' said Selina.

'You sound confident,' said Perry. 'Did you sit and discuss business then, outside of swimming?'

'We had lunch and then we had dinner.'

'Well, I had dinner with him,' said Selina. 'You were having to go for your appointment.'

'Yes, but I caught you up at the end of dinner,' said Carmen.

'What did you discuss at dinner?' asked Perry.

'In truth, we were really done by then. He's quite an entertainer, though. Quite a talker,' said Selina.

Perry thought he saw rather anxious eyes from Carmen when that statement was made. He glanced across at Ross. He remained impassive, and Perry wondered if his boss had picked up on that too.

'Had you signed papers to go ahead?' asked Ross.

63

'We gave a conditional yes,' said Selina. 'You had to get the paperwork all through and that. He was giving a conditional yes, too. They would check out our backgrounds and whether we were good for it. Standard business practice.'

'And how soon are you looking to get into this?' asked Perry.

'Soon as. We're not working at the moment. We've got a few bits of savings, but we need to get going,' said Carmen.

'The house owned or rented?' asked Perry. Selina drew back a minute from this question, but Carmen answered past her.

'We're renting at the moment. We have enough money, but we didn't want to lay down roots to find it wasn't where we wanted. It's not really how we would envision a house. We could do with setting our own mark on it. But, as the business goes ahead, we might look to purchase our own set-up.'

'Did you ever see Stephen Ludlow when you were swimming competitively?' Perry asked Carmen.

'See, yes. Spoke to, talked to, no. I mean, he was a fantastic swimmer. Absolutely fantastic. Model of how to get in shape and how to do it.'

'You've obviously kept a lot of your own sporting prowess,' said Perry. He looked at her legs. They weren't just bare, they were toned, definitely muscular. This was a woman who'd worked out, who could do sports. Glancing across at Selina, she didn't have the same build. It wasn't that she wasn't good looking—she was; she was an attractive young woman—but she didn't have the muscular look.

'Do you know what car he was driving?' asked Perry.

'Black hire car,' said Selina. 'It was definitely a hire car. He took me to dinner in it because Carmen was then to pick me up in her car, and it was immaculate. People don't have cars like that—everybody's car has a bit of dirt around it—unless

64

you own a really impressive car. In that case, maybe, but this, this was just a basic hire car.'

'And did he say anything about any of the other franchises?' asked Ross.

'He told us he'd met with them,' said Carmen. 'But he was impressed with ours. To be honest, I think he would have sold franchises to everybody. He wouldn't be bothered as long as you were bringing enough numbers. He was there to make money at the end of the day.'

'Just like yourselves,' said Perry.

'Quite,' said Selina.

'Was there anything that he said that showed whether he had any problems, or had anybody following him, or he had a difficulty with anyone?' asked Ross.

'Not at all,' said Carmen.

'What was he like as a person?' asked Perry. 'Was he businesslike or was he more . . .?'

'He was quite intimate,' said Selina. Again, the eyes of Carmen flashed an annoyed look. She may not have appreciated that.

'Intimate?' said Perry. 'In what way?'

'Well, at dinner. He was quite . . . well, he paid a few compliments,' said Selina. 'Not the sort of things you would say to a business client.'

'Such as?' asked Ross.

'He complimented my dress, said it showed off my figure, said it was impressive. Actually mentioned how good my bottom looked in it—he didn't say bottom; he said another word.'

'Was he like that during the day?' asked Perry.

'He did compliment Carmen when she was in her wetsuit.'

'Said I would attract the men. With my . . . he said with my breasts,' said Carmen. 'In truth, I didn't find him particularly professional in that sense.'

'Did you pull him up on it?' asked Perry.

'No,' said Carmen. 'He said little afterwards because I didn't exactly warm to the comment. So, I think he got the idea that I wasn't interested.'

'But he commented about you later on?' confirmed Perry to Selina.

'He did, not that it meant anything to me. Maybe he's one of these guys—you hear about these businessmen, don't you? They're away from home—see what they can get. He was in very good shape, though. Outstanding figure. Hadn't lost it from his competitive days,' said Selina.

'And what did he do when he left you?' asked Ross.

'Well, we left him at the restaurant. Carmen was there. We came back here, went to bed. Yesterday, we've been down to the shore. We were filling in forms, looking through more of the paperwork. We did our shopping yesterday, too.'

'Did you go out at all that night or either of the last two nights into the water?'

'No,' said Selina. 'It's freezing. What sort of idiot would go out there?'

'Exactly,' said Carmen. 'We've been in here. We don't like the cold particularly. I've got the best drysuit you can buy for when I go out there. Especially at this time of year. It's not like back in Spain or even down in South America. You can get into the water in your bikini or swimsuit. You wouldn't do that here. It's freezing.'

'Got to be insane,' confirmed Selina.

'Well,' said Perry, 'plenty of Scottish people would jump in.

But then again, I guess we're just made for it. Some of us have extra layers around us. It helps.' He gave a slap onto his belly, and that made Carmen laugh. Ross glanced over.

'Well, if that's all,' he said to Perry, 'I think we'll call it a day. Are you going anywhere in the near future?' asked Ross.

'No, like I said, we're here,' said Carmen. 'Well, we need to know what happens now with the franchise, whether that goes ahead. That'll dictate what happens. Or we might have to look to see if there's another one. Or can we run it on our own? It's kind of put a bit of a stick in the works.'

'I can see that,' said Ross. 'Well, thank you for your time, and we'll be in contact if we need you.'

Perry left with Ross, and stepped out into the cold to feel his cheeks burning. He threw his coat around him again, quickly. As he sat back in the car, he watched as Selina waved from the door to them, Carmen again hanging over her shoulder.

'Lovers, friends, business colleagues, what do you reckon?' said Perry.

'I didn't think Selina has the same opinion of what relationship they have as Carmen,' said Ross.

'Exactly,' said Perry. 'Carmen didn't like his comments either. Selina didn't seem to mind them. I'm wondering if there was a bit of jealousy there.'

'There's nothing to say she did anything.'

'No, there isn't. I'm just trying to understand the situation. Just—'

'Hypothesising,' said Ross. 'That's all it was. We've got no evidence of anything at the moment. Let's head back, meet the boss, see what he says. I need to get in to having a look on the computer too. Check out who these people are. Or make sure they are who they say they are.'

'And I need to do some more hypothesising,' said Perry. He gave a smile as he caught the look Ross was giving him.

Chapter 08

Macleod went to see Jona, who was now back on the scene. She had nothing further to advise on Stephen Ludlow's body. He hadn't drowned. He'd been killed with a knife in the back—a serrated knife and performed by someone who knew how to kill him quickly from behind. The blade had been driven into precisely the right area.

Were they looking at a hit? The thought had crossed Macleod's mind. But to have a hit taken out on you, there had to be reasons. Like every murder, the story needed to be told—to find out who the man had crossed in his life, who the man had angered so much that he was now dead.

The cave had the boys' DNA in it. It had Stephen Ludlow's DNA in it. The body had scraped across bits of rocks, and Jona had picked up small bits of flesh. His hair was there, too, but nothing else was discovered.

Macleod had been hoping that the cave might have thrown up some other answers, shown some other intruder. Even if they hadn't known who that intruder was from either DNA or other bodily secretions, it would have offered them something. There had been no sign either that Stephen Ludlow had sex before his death, according to Jona, but that would have fitted. If Gail Harmon had sex with him on a previous day, as reported by Perry and Ross, then he would have been washed up by the time he actually died.

Macleod was at the beginning of an investigation—that part where you drew in all the parts of the story, but the story was in no shape. You couldn't tell the story when some of it was missing. Trying to piece a story together on the go was always difficult, always frustrating. But he'd been at this job for so long now, he knew to be patient and he knew to bring his team together.

He let them have a few hours to work. Around about midnight, Macleod brought them back together in the recesses of Thurso Police Station. There was strong coffee on the go, for he wasn't sure how long they'd be up tonight.

'Right, then,' said Macleod, marching into the room. 'You've all had a while, so let's get together. Make sure we know what each other knows.'

He sat down, waiting for the rest of the team to assemble around a small table. He liked it when it was a small number. Big meetings were difficult to handle. Small ones were politer, more efficient.

'You want to kick us off, Ross?' said Macleod to his sergeant.

'Very good, sir,' said Ross. 'I've done a search through all the owners. I cannot find any financial irregularities with any of them,' said Ross. 'They've not been in trouble with the banks. They've not been turned down for loans. So, as business prospects, they all look quite good. However,' said Ross, 'I've been struggling to get more information on Carmen Cabral. I'll need to look further into her.'

'Unusual to not find any more?' asked Macleod.

'I wouldn't say that yet,' said Ross. 'I'll let you know.'

'What else have we got, Perry?' Macleod asked.

'I've been looking into the death of Gail Harmon's husband,' said Perry. 'He died out at sea. The official report said it was drowning, but it was strange.'

'In what way?' asked Macleod.

'Well, it doesn't say it was suspicious, except for the fact he was a competent swimmer. In fact, more than a competent swimmer. He was, like many people seem to be in this case, a competitive wild swimmer. However, he died out at sea. Couldn't find any reason, couldn't find a struggle, just found he drowned while out swimming.'

'When you say they didn't find a struggle,' said Macleod, 'what do you mean by that exactly?'

'Well, they say he may have struggled as he was drowning, but there was nothing forced on him. There were no marks on the body to say he was under any sort of outside pressure.'

'And should that be the case?' asked Macleod.

'Well, he wasn't hit in the head,' said Perry. 'I suppose if you held him under the water, it won't always show up.'

'But the death's suspicious?' said Macleod.

'It's not reported as suspicious. He just drowned. They just can't find out why he would drown. Maybe he got a cramp, but there's nothing showing that in the autopsy either. He got himself into difficulties and drowned, is what the coroner down in England said.'

'So, unknown?'

'Yeah,' said Perry. 'Unknown, really. Surprising.'

'Surprising.' Macleod looked over at Susan Cunningham. She was sitting with one leg up on a chair. 'You okay?' he asked.

'Takes a bit of getting used to the prosthetic,' she said. 'You get a bit of pain every now and again. It's like walking on a whole new piece. You walk with no feeling below. And yet, sometimes I feel like my leg is coming back. I feel like my leg is still there. It's weird.'

'I'm sure it is,' said Macleod. 'But you're okay?'

'Will be. I'm getting about and certainly not feeling the need to be removed from duty or anything.'

'But what have you found?' he asked.

'Well, Perry mentioned it, everybody in this case seems to be a competitive swimmer. So I thought I should look up about them. One thing I found was unusual; Achterberg's daughter, Abby. Abby was a competitor. She finished just as Gail started competing.'

'Did she get anywhere, this Abigail Achterberg?'

'Junior events and stuff. But she's not really getting to a level that's highly competitive, unlike Gail, who did and then met her husband from it. Gail was quite good until her husband died and then she withdrew.'

'Did you get anything on Carmen Cabral?' asked Perry.

'She must have been competing overseas,' said Susan, 'because she's not competing in the UK. Can't find her in any race listings.'

'She definitely looks a swimmer,' said Perry. 'Unlike her friend, partner, or whatever she is, Selina.'

'She was odd too,' said Ross. 'We arrived, Carmen was, well, she looked like she'd got out of the bath or something, wearing a dressing gown. The house was blazing with heat. I guess that's the climate they're more used to. But she was wearing, well, I would have said it was inappropriate for having two men come into the house.'

'She didn't want to change then?' said Macleod. 'I mean, are you sure it was inappropriate?'

'Susan,' said Ross, 'if two police constables you didn't know came to interview you, and you'd just got out of the bath into a—well, shortish dressing gown—would you go and change?'

'Absolutely,' said Susan, 'unless they were great looking.' She gave a cheeky smile.

'But seriously,' said Ross.

'Of course I would, and I'm not just saying that because I'm sitting with my boss.'

'Something else,' said Perry. 'I noticed Carmen is a bit fonder of Selina than Selina seemed to be of Carmen.'

'Well, yes, to a point,' said Ross.

'Beyond a point,' said Perry. 'I don't know if you picked up on it. Every time Selina spoke about Ludlow, Carmen reacted. Carmen wasn't happy. Anyway, Selina went off on her own to dinner with him.'

'Right,' said Macleod. 'And that was because . . .?'

'Carmen had an appointment. So, I don't think it was premeditated,' said Perry. 'I think, though, that Carmen was bothered. That's why I asked about their relationship. They didn't turn around and say we're partners. I mean, Ross, if you and Angus were out, and they said, "What's the deal with you two?" You would say we're partners. We're in a relationship, yes?'

'These days, yes, I would. I wouldn't have previously, but yes, these days.'

'Exactly. You're proud of your relationship. That's great,' said Perry. 'But these two? Selina doesn't even talk like they're in one. Carmen, meanwhile, is hanging all over Selina. And it's weird. She's hugging her, but she's getting no response.'

'Some people don't respond,' said Ross.

'No, that's not right,' said Perry. 'People respond. In their own way, they respond. If your partner gives you a hug, you will respond. You might turn round and be annoyed at them, in which case you'll show it. There'll be an inflexion. There'll be something to show it. But Selina was almost ignoring it, as if it's just nothing. The difference between girlfriends and partners.'

'You sure about that?' said Macleod.

'I am. Susan, you know what I mean, don't you? If a girlfriend came up and gave you a hug from behind, you wouldn't react back into it. But if a bloke you wanted, if a bloke you liked did it, or if a bloke you really didn't like did it, you'd react. You'd move either towards or away.'

'I guess so,' said Susan.

'I don't know what it means,' said Perry. 'I don't understand their relationship.'

'Well, keep an eye on it then,' said Macleod. 'But what have we got at the moment? We've got three franchises. The first one, the Achterbergs, they seem to be quite happy to set up. They've had a daughter that's previously done competitive swimming. He's military.'

'So that could tie him to the blade and to the killing. He'd be capable of it,' said Susan.

'Yes, but capability doesn't mean he did,' said Macleod. 'We haven't got a reason for him to do it at the moment.'

'No,' said Perry, 'we don't. In fact, you'd have to ask why. What's the point? He wants the business.'

'Exactly,' said Macleod, 'but they all do. Gail Harmon, she's gone to bed with him. She seemed to be very happy about that, according to you two, earlier.'

'She was,' said Perry. 'She's visibly upset he's dead. Gail struck me as incredibly insecure, though. After the death of her husband, she finally had time to see somebody she liked, somebody she got really got close to. Gail jumped in with both feet, and didn't seem to regret it either prior to his death. Her regret now is more that he's gone than anything else. Also quite shocked, though, he lied to her.'

'So, she was vulnerable,' said Macleod.

'Sounds like it,' said Susan. 'You can get like that. I know, I've been there, just wanting to be liked, just wanting that closeness and you end up with nothing.' There was a bitterness in her voice and then the silence took over the room.

'Past all that now though,' said Macleod. 'We live and learn.'

'Yes,' said Susan. 'But I understand where she's coming from.'

'Any chance she would have known, though, that he was seeing someone beforehand?' asked Macleod. 'If that was the case, she'd have a good reason for killing him.'

'Her reaction was genuine, I believe,' said Perry.

'I concur,' said Ross. 'It seemed genuine.'

'So again, she's got no reason to kill him, then,' said Macleod. 'If that's the case, we then go on to our third business. We don't know a lot about their past. Maybe that's worth looking into. Carmen is meant to be a competitive swimmer, but not here. We need to find out what these two have come from. But there seems to be no reason. Well, maybe Carmen's jealous of him. But jealous enough to go out and kill? Why? He hasn't slept with Selina.'

'As far as we know,' said Susan. 'He's got form for women.'

'Selina didn't seem that interested in him,' said Perry. 'She didn't seem bothered by his death, except for the business. Selina's the one that looks comfortable; Carmen's the one that's not.'

'It'd be a bit of a jump to see somebody as a threat and just go out and kill them before they've even done anything. You'd have to be what? Not quite there,' said Ross.

'It does seem extreme,' said Macleod. 'But if it's not somebody up here, then it needs to be further back in his past.'

'What about Tabby?' asked Susan.

'She doesn't seem to be much of a suspect at the moment,' said Macleod.

'No,' said Susan. 'But Ludlow did the dirty on her. If Ludlow's doing the dirty on her, and she founds out, she could kill. I know I would.'

For a moment, the men in the room stopped and looked at her.

'What? Well, you would. You would. That's what it is, isn't it? There's nothing so angry as a woman scorned,' said Susan. 'It's true. We don't forgive quickly.'

They remained quiet again until Ross said, 'It makes me glad I'm made the way I am.'

Laughter burst out and Macleod was quite impressed. He'd never seen that side of Ross. Such a quick wit. But he was also growing more comfortable talking about his sexuality in front of people. Macleod knew it had always bothered Ross in front of Macleod. And in truth, in the past, Macleod wouldn't have been someone who had accepted it well. Times had changed and Ross was a decent officer, and a good man. Any hang-up was Macleod's problem now, not Ross's.

'Well then, let's get into the background of this lot. Ross, I also want to know more about Ludlow. I want to know about this business of his. I want to know what's going on further south. We need to understand more about him. If there's somebody coming after him from further afield, we're nowhere with finding that out at the moment.'

'Sir,' said Ross.

'Let's also make sure we find out about Carmen. Too much we don't know about her and Selina. Let's get the goods on them. Check these businesses out more thoroughly. It seems bizarre that somebody would go to all the trouble of putting this man in a cave. Getting out to the cave would be the modus of somebody who could operate a boat or get out there swimming.'

'Maybe to meet him,' said Susan. 'It would be ideal if you were a wild water swimmer, a strong one. Great place to meet, nobody else to come near you. And afterwards you could just say you were out for a midnight swim.'

'Yes,' said Macleod. 'Not something I've ever gone for.' He heard a noise at the door. A knocking sound.

'That's somebody, come on in,' said Macleod.

A young female constable opened the door. 'Call for Detective Chief Inspector Macleod,' she said.

'That's me, Seoras. You are?'

'Constable Lennox.'

'What's your first name, Lennox?' asked Macleod.

'Annie.'

'Thank you, Annie. Where's the easiest place to take the call?'

'This way, this way.' It was like she was trying to think what she should say.

'This way, Seoras,' said Macleod. He stood up and followed the young girl. She led him through to the front desk where he picked up the phone. 'This is Macleod.'

'This is the Coastguard. Aberdeen Station. I thought I'd let you know. They said that you were dealing with the body we found the other day.'

'I am. What's up?'

'We got an observation from a fishing vessel who thought they saw a body in the water. We have the lifeboat out and some others doing a quick search. Given the circumstances, we thought we should call you up.'

'Okay,' said Macleod. 'Well, let me know if you find something.'

'That's the thing—we just have. We've got a young male in the water. Where are you currently, sir?'

'I'm in Thurso.'

'If you make your way back down towards Port Skye, in fact, go down towards one of the quays down there and we'll get the lifeboat to bring it in.'

'Have you got a contact for our forensic team from the last time?' asked Macleod.

'We have.'

'Get the lifeboat to contact Jona Nakamura. She'll deal with the body coming ashore. Very good, thank you,' said Macleod. He put the phone down and walked back to the office.

'Ross, into the computers, we just had a body found. Perry, why don't you come with me? Susan, you stay here, nurse that leg up a bit, see what else you can find in the backgrounds of these people. I'll give you a shout when we know who the body is, or anything about it.'

Perry picked up his jacket following Macleod out the door. As they went down the corridor, Macleod looked over his shoulder. 'Carmen Cabral,' he said to Perry. 'You reckon she could have?'

'I very much reckon she could have. I've no evidence to say she did, though.'

Macleod nodded. Evidence. That was the trouble. Start of investigation, you had all the ideas, you had all the beliefs, you had all your feelings, and you had no evidence.

Chapter 09

Macleod stood in the back of the forensic wagon with Jona Nakamura. She was dressed in her coverall outfit, having seen the body and planning for it to be taken away.

'He was naked,' said Jona. 'Completely naked. Lifeboat found him, picked him up, brought him back.'

'Have you got any initial thoughts on how he died?'

'Well,' said Jona, 'there's a nice hole in his back. Looks like a serrated knife has gone in. It appears very similar to how Ludlow died. I can't confirm that yet, though. Obviously, because he's been in the sea, I need to get him back to the lab to have a proper look. But at the moment, that's what seems.'

'What's the Coastguard said about where this body's probably come from?'

'According to the tides, it might have come back in off the coast. It's not an exact science. And they don't know how long he's been in the water. I would say only a day or two at most.'

'So, it's going to be a while before we get any more information?'

'Not exactly,' said Jona, 'or maybe.'

'What's that meant to mean?'

'One of the local officers, he saw the body when it came in. He thought it looked like someone. He's off chasing that up.'

'Someone?'

'One of the kids in the local area,' said Jona, 'hadn't come home. No big deal about it. Parents just thought they were hanging out with somebody else.'

'So, what? Is he definitely missing?'

'I don't know. Sent the constable off to chase it up. Thought that was best.'

'Fair enough,' said Macleod. 'What else are we doing?'

'Well, they thought they should check the rest of the coast. The search coordinator's doing that at the moment. They've got Coastguard rescue teams combing the coast. They've got the lifeboat going back and forward with its Y-boat, up along the edges. Search is continuing at the moment, in case he was with someone.'

'How long are they going to do that for?'

'Not very long,' said Jona. 'I've told them it looks like he was killed. I believe they're just covering off the last of the search area.'

Macleod nodded, stepped out of the wagon, and stood, looking out towards the sea. The lifeboat wasn't that far away at the moment. He could see the lights of it, and the little Y-boat going back and forward. They seemed to be busy.

The search coordinator was along from them, working at the back of one of the vans. Macleod knew better than to disturb him. They were busy. When they found something they'd come to him. Besides, they were working with Jona at the moment, who was probably the best contact to have. Susan could take over soon. She had a lot of experience of working with search teams.

He could feel the cold in his hands despite the gloves that he wore. His coat was wrapped up around him. He had a scarf on as well, and instead of a fedora hat, he had a beanie. He didn't like beanies normally, but in this weather, you had to wear them. Macleod shivered. Once again, somebody had tossed somebody into the water.

'Inspector!' came a shout. It came from the search wagons. One of the men on the radio there was waving Macleod over. He was the one coordinating the search.

Macleod turned and shouted towards the forensic wagon, 'Jona, do you want to come?'

Jona burst out from the wagon, still in her coverall uniform. Macleod waited for her before walking over to the small group of vehicles that comprised the hub of the search.

'Miss Nakamura, Detective Chief Inspector, one of our teams has just found something.'

'What?' asked Macleod.

'There's a cave down here, smaller than the one the boys saw that previous body in. Not much of a cave at all, but there's a cave down here. There's a lot of clothing there.'

'What sort of clothing?' asked Macleod.

'They're taking some photographs of it. Miss Nakamura, did you want one of your people down there? You can get access to it.'

'Go on, Jona, get down there,' said Macleod. 'I'll get a coverall on, come down with you.'

He looked around for Perry and saw the man on the phone.

'Perry, coverall on. They found something.'

Perry nodded and came over towards the wagons. It took Macleod and Perry about ten minutes before they were suited up with Wellingtons, coveralls over as much of their clothing as they could muster. One of the search team took Macleod down to the front of the wagon. They were able to get him from the wagon, down across to the cliff edge, and worked down gently across rocks until they approached the cave.

'If you watch your footing coming round here, you can get in easily enough,' said the search team member accompanying Macleod.

'Miss Nakamura!' shouted the man. A minute later, Jona's face came out of the cave.

'You can come in, Inspector,' she said. 'You too, Perry; just watch your footing.'

Slowly Macleod made his way into the cave. There weren't a lot of places to stand, but he saw a ledge on one side and an amount of clothing there. Jona was going through it carefully, having photographed everything.

'You found something?' he asked.

'Wallet in here. It's got a credit card. Danny Poland is the name on it. Seventeen,' Jona said. 'I think that might have been the young man that our constable went off to see about.'

'Why has he got clothing here?' said Macleod.

'I think there might have been somebody else here,' said Jona. 'Or somewhere else. He's got an empty condom packet.'

'Is there a sheath left around?' said Perry.

'A what?' said Jona.

'Condom. Sheath. Used one.'

'Not that I've found,' said Jona. 'And to be honest . . . really? In here?'

Perry looked around. 'He's seventeen according to the wallet. He might have had a young girl with him. I mean, that age, going somewhere where you can hide out, where you can—'

'Seriously, Perry,' said Macleod. 'It's freezing. You wouldn't.'

'Well, I wouldn't,' said Perry, 'but you never know what people do.'

'Any indication the body was in here?' asked Macleod. 'Slipped into the water?'

'You mean did somebody plant the clothes here and were going to hide the body as well? No, not that I can tell. No indication that it wasn't either, though. It's one of those things. We'll look into it, but it's going to be hard to prove that.'

Macleod nodded. He turned to one of the search advisors. 'What's the likelihood the body could have come from this cave?'

'It's within tidal patterns, but to be honest, that's a shot in the dark. We're saying that it could have come from anywhere along this coast. Could have been dropped out at sea. It's not that exact a science. You can't trace it back to one single spot. And when you use the modelling, it says it came from here, but that's with a massive degree of probability around it. Safer to say an area.'

Macleod nodded again. 'Danny Poland,' he said out loud. 'Danny Poland. Why a seventeen-year-old from here?' He turned to Perry. 'We've got a dead man who comes from nowhere near here. He's looking to set up wild swimming. And now we've got a youth dead. Why?'

'Bottles of wine here,' said Perry in response. 'Not opened.'

'Any signs of being disturbed?' asked Macleod.

'Wine's just sitting there. I'll get on to this, Inspector,' said Jona. 'I'll get the lights up with a proper recce on everything else in here. It's going to be hard to pull out evidence and that, though. I'll see what I can find.'

Macleod nodded. 'Load the photos and that up in the usual places.' Carefully, he made his way back up the cliff. His bones were aching and Macleod was frozen to the core.

'What now?' said Perry.

'What time do you make it, Perry?'

'Three in the morning.'

'Do you know of anywhere that's got a coffee?' asked Macleod.

'Apart from the station?'

'We need to find out about this Danny Poland. Get on to the station, see where that officer's gone.'

Perry nodded, picked up his phone, and went into the forensic van to make the call. Macleod, meanwhile, went back to the car. He switched on the engine and put on the blow heater, hoping to warm up.

Macleod sighed. He thought about phoning Jane, but it would be unfair to call her at three in the morning. She knew where he was, knew what he was doing. She always said don't bother to call unless he had time. This was his job; this is what he did, but it had been a while since he'd been in charge like this.

He looked along the road. He could see that the police had made a cordon. Beyond it now were the press—they'd have heard about this. It wasn't difficult. Rescues and searches happened over radio waves, and while coastguards and police officers were careful about what they said, there was only so much you could cover up. The body had come ashore, after all. Forensic wagons were there. He'd have to speak to them soon. That was something he was missing. He didn't have anyone else to deal with it. He could ask Ross to do it.

But in truth, Ross wasn't the person. Perry didn't look good. And Susan wasn't experienced enough with the press. You had to keep a tight lid on them, and you had to keep them at a

85

distance at the same time as trying to use them when you could. Hope was very adept at it. She had a good relationship with them. But then again, they all liked Hope. Who could blame them? Tall, red-headed woman. And now she was pregnant.

When the bump started to show, the press would lap that up too. He was just the grumpy git of an inspector. They'd turned on him several times. 'Macleod hadn't found this; Macleod hadn't found that. What was Macleod doing?' He didn't hate the press, but he did loathe them. There were some good people there, some proper journalists, but a lot of them were making noise out of nothing.

And to Macleod, that was just disrespectful and unhelpful. He was going to switch the light on in the car, because he didn't like the darkness. But he knew then the press would get a photograph of him sitting in the car, chilled and cold. Hope wouldn't look chilled and cold. She would look impressive, strutting about, organising this and that.

He shook his head. When was he ever competing against Hope? Why did he start thinking it was nice she wasn't here? Was he just becoming a dinosaur and afraid of the upcoming competition?

Perry was wandering back over. He saw Macleod in the car and got in beside him.

'What's the deal, Perry?' asked Macleod.

'Danny Poland. Officer's there at the moment, breaking the news. I think we'll need to head over.'

'What's the story?'

'Seventeen-year-old gone out. Often he doesn't come back for a night or two. He's got a girlfriend as well, they reckon. Or at least he's had a couple in the past.'

'Any names?'

'He's a quiet lad, in some ways. But I'm not sure. I said we'll be over. Talk to the parents. Thought you'd want to do that straight away.'

'Of course,' said Macleod. 'We will do. How far is it?'

'Won't take us more than about ten minutes.'

'Go in the other direction for ten minutes first,' said Macleod. 'And then back.'

'Why?' said Perry.

'Well,' said Macleod, 'I could tell you it's because I want the press to see us going off in a different direction, so that we arrive quietly at the parents' house. But I want ten minutes of this car getting heated up, and another ten minutes to enjoy it before I get to that house. Otherwise, I'm going to walk in like some sort of iceman.'

Perry gave a smile. 'I don't get it, though,' he said. 'Why a young lad? If it had been one of the other business partners—the potential business partners—I would have seen it as something within the case. But this guy, I mean, who is he? He's a kid.'

'The other kids found the body, though, didn't they?' said Macleod.

'What, you think our killer might think this guy saw something? Found it?' said Perry.

'I wonder how smoothly things went,' said Macleod, 'when they killed him. They or he, she, or whoever. How open was it? Did they meet somewhere? What do they know about the kids?'

'Do you want me to—?'

'Yes,' said Macleod quietly. 'See if we can get some officers to be near the others at the moment. Tell them not to leave the house.'

'To be honest, I don't think the parents are going to let them out of the house after that stunt they pulled.'

'Advise them, properly,' said Macleod. 'Get Susan to do that.'

Perry nodded and picked up his phone. While he spoke to Susan Cunningham, Macleod sat and wondered. The trouble with a murder was that it could snowball. You committed one murder to get rid of one problem. Then you saw the next problem. If you've committed murder once, committing it twice to solve a problem is no problem at all. You become adept.

It becomes the solution that you go to straight away rather than the solution that is forced upon you. Is that what was happening here? Macleod hoped not. He gave a sigh.

Macleod made sure that all the dials were turned up to hot for the air to blow. He took off his gloves and put his hands where the air was blowing through, but it was still cold. Only when they started driving would the hot air truly come through.

'Ten minutes, you say, the other direction,' said Perry.

'Ten minutes,' said Macleod. 'Get some heat into this old body of mine.'

He understood now why some people smoked, especially on cold nights like this. Still, filthy habit. The joy of Inverness was you could probably find a coffee at this time of night.

He'd need to make some flasks up, to travel around with them. That was one thing for the next meeting. He found himself just talking. Talking to put off his thoughts about the ncxt meeting he was going to have. Talking to the parents of deceased children was never something you got used to.

Chapter 10

Macleod approached the doorstep of the Poland household with a touch of trepidation. He had seen a lot in his time, but when you had to approach newly bereaved parents, there was nothing that prepared you for it. It never got any easier. Never got any less painful.

There would be shock, there would be disbelief, and there would possibly be anger. There would just be loss. And it was one side of Macleod's job he did not like.

He almost felt guilty at times like these, because his job was what he was good at, and he enjoyed his job. Working out what was going on, who was doing what, how they were scheming, how they were ahead of the game was a delight. He enjoyed bringing them in.

But he didn't enjoy this, and he didn't enjoy the fact something like this had to happen before he went to his job, before he could be a detective. If there were no murders, he'd have no job. Jane had told him it wasn't his fault that there were murders, but he still felt a little guilty at enjoying his job too much.

Macleod rang the doorbell, and it was answered by a young

constable. Her eyes were sullen, and she turned and looked up at him. 'I'm glad you're here, sir,' she said.

Macleod wondered how they did it, sitting for such long periods of time with bereaved families. What could you offer them? It wasn't like you were a minister or someone of faith who could go in and give some comfort, at least if the bereaved were of the religious bent. But then again, even that was cold.

His faith had struggled when his wife had died, his own relationship with God ripped asunder. Macleod wasn't one for swearing, but he told God to go away in that coarser form. It was a word he never used.

Maybe that was the problem. Maybe it was the death of others, of loved ones, that brought it back to him and the loss he'd suffered. He always thought it was strange that Jane never took that pain away. Not that he was complaining about her. It wasn't any lack of effort on her own part. Just that, well, the loss of his first wife was not something you got over. It was something that was always there. And as wonderful as Jane was, and as terrific as his life had been with her, that hurt you just learned to live with.

You didn't learn to get over it. Neither would these parents.

Macleod entered a living room with Perry to see a man holding a woman close to him. There was a younger sibling in the far corner who looked almost shell-shocked. The young female constable went beside the teenager, while Macleod sat in a chair close to the parents.

There was no chair for Perry, but he stood without a word.

'My name's DCI Seoras Macleod. This is Detective Constable Warren Perry. First, can I offer my condolences at your loss? I'm so very sorry.'

The woman didn't look up, but the man did and simply gave

a nod.

'My apologies. I have to ask you questions at a time like this. Quite possibly the last thing you need. But, unfortunately, I do if I'm going to have any chance of bringing Danny's killers to justice. It looks like he was murdered.'

'Murdered?' said the woman in disbelief.

'I'm afraid so,' said Macleod. 'Sylvia, isn't it?'

She had her head back down again, but the man had raised his and nodded. 'I'm James. This is my wife, Sylvia. That's Alice over there—Danny's sister.'

'I need to establish,' said Macleod, 'Danny's movements, where he's been. I'll also need to look in his room and possibly round the rest of the house, just so I can find any clues as to what's going on.'

'Of course,' said James.

But Sylvia looked up with a hard face. 'Don't! Don't disturb his stuff. Don't. It's all I have now. It's all I've—'

'I won't,' said Macleod. 'If I need to take anything, we'll bring it back. We won't hold on to it forever.'

He knew he could hold on to it for quite a while if it was evidence in the case. And he would not promise he could have it back the next day. But he didn't want to make the woman suffer any more than she had.

'Can you tell me a little about Danny's last movements? Where he's been the last few days? What you know?'

Sylvia wept, and James pulled her close. Sylvia was a small woman, probably in her fifties, and James, a slightly taller man, with wide shoulders, and hair that was moving backwards on the top of his head. His eyes were sullen, having obviously cried himself, but he was forcing himself to answer.

'Danny was quite aloof. He's been in that teenage phase,' said

James. 'Doesn't really talk to you. Everything's quite snappy. Not a bad kid, at least he wasn't. He, well, he had his mates he liked to go out and see. They would kick about. Sometimes they'd say there's not much to do around here. Go round the coast, you'd see them down at the beaches sometimes. James. Not so much of late, because it's gone a lot colder.'

'But his mates don't know where they've been?'

'The first people we contacted. They hadn't seen him.'

'He attended a local school?' asked Macleod.

'Yes, he's not a great academic. But he was getting his qualifications. He was going to be all right, would get enough,' said his father. 'He went with his friends a couple of days ago. But he'd left them. We checked. They didn't know where he was going. He said he was going elsewhere. He'd been very quiet about it. Not sure why. He only met with them briefly.'

'But he would have been out that night. The night after. He'd been gone before for a night or two. Always crashed at his mates. He was rubbish at telling you where he was. But you don't want to push them at this age, do you? You don't want to get on top of them. You don't want to push them away.'

'I understand,' said Macleod. 'I'm not here to judge about anything that happened. I just need to know what happened. This is so I can work out what happened to Danny.'

'He seemed happy, though, the last lot of days. Didn't leave a note,' said James. 'He was—'

'He was happy,' said Sylvia. 'Happier than I'd seen him for a long while. Buzzing. He was . . . there was something about him. I think there was someone. He was different. Didn't go out the door in an angry mood. He was actually happy.

'He did the dishes for me. Cleared the dishes away before he went out. If he was in the mood, he wouldn't have done that.'

Macleod looked over at Alice. 'Did he tell you anything, Alice?'

She shook her head.

'Alice and Danny didn't speak that much,' said James.

'How long would have been abnormal for him to have been away?' asked Perry.

'I think if he had been out another night, we'd have called you,' said James. 'Started asking a bit more strongly. He's seventeen. They're meant to be able to take care of themselves now, aren't they? Sixteen-year-old is an adult these days. Thought he was out with his mates. They look after each other. Not bad kids, you know. They do look after each other.'

'We found his clothing,' said Macleod. 'And we found a used condom. Or rather, an open packet. Do you know if he was seeing anyone?'

Sylvia looked up, tears in her eyes. 'I don't know,' she said, 'but that would explain it. He, well . . . he was that age, wasn't he? Teenage boy. Hormones. He had pictures in his room, you know. That's what they do at that age. Not . . . not dirty pictures. Pictures of women. Models and such like. Just a normal kid,' said Sylvia. 'Just a normal kid. How does . . .'

Macleod gave her a moment as Sylvia wept bitterly into her husband's shoulder. After the moment had passed, he said, 'Do you mind if I go upstairs and have a look at his room?'

'No,' said James. 'Of course not. If you go up the stairs, his is the second on the right.'

'I can show you,' said Sylvia.

'No, no,' said Macleod. 'It's okay. You stay here. I'll have a look. Constable, stay here too. Thank you. Perry, with me.'

Macleod gave an almost apologetic nod and left the room before climbing the stairs. There were pictures of two young children in the hall and then older pairs of children as they climbed the stairs.

This was the hard bit. He saw a family with history. It wasn't just a body sitting on a mortuary slab. This was a life. This was a person. Especially when it was young. He never got past it. So much potential.

Macleod saw a young lad in a football strip. He saw a family at Disneyland. He saw someone canoeing, people swimming, people on the beach.

When they reached the room of Danny Poland, Macleod opened it, allowed Perry in, and then closed the door behind him.

'What do you make of him?' asked Macleod.

'Pretty normal by the looks of it,' said Perry. 'Sad.'

'It is,' said Macleod. He looked at the room around him. There was a desk with a computer on it. Above it was a large poster. It was a woman in a bikini. There were several other women in swimwear. There were also some music posters up. Album covers. People from bands on stage. Macleod could see nothing particularly unusual.

He pulled open drawers and found clothing. One drawer held a lot of pens and pencils. Schoolwork in another. The school bag was lying in the corner. There was a football strip as well in one, and some football pictures on the wall. *Just a normal kid*, thought Macleod. There was a small drawer at the top of the desk unit, and pulling it back, he saw some receipts. Several were from a while ago.

One seemed to be for a controller for the Xbox. Another one was for a mobile phone. That seemed to be missing. It wasn't in the clothing they had found. But if you're anywhere sensible as a killer, you've switched it off and thrown it away.

Hard to trace it. He looked through some of the other receipts. Two of them were recent. Very recent.

'Here, Perry,' said Macleod.

There was a receipt for the supermarket. Several bottles of wine. Chocolates too. There was also a receipt for a jeweller in Thurso. Macleod picked up his phone to contact Jona.

'Jona, I'm at the house of Danny Poland's parents. I've got a receipt from his bedroom. See the wine you found near the clothing? What was it?'

'Supermarket-owned brand. It was a red, Chilean red. We have a rosé and a sparkling white.'

'Pinot Noir sparkling?' said Macleod.

'Yes. Why do you ask?'

'I've found the receipts for them in his room,' said Macleod. 'He's obviously gone and prepared for this meeting, wherever he was going. Was there a bag with the bottles?'

'No,' said Jona. 'Just the bottles.'

'I've also found a receipt for a jeweller in Thurso. I'll get there first thing in the morning. Are there any items of jewellery on his clothing or body?'

'No,' said Jona. 'None at all.'

'I think he was there to meet someone,' said Macleod. 'Either that or he had met someone before he was disturbed.'

'If I may, sir,' said Perry. 'Perhaps he was setting up the meet. And then met her somewhere else to take her to the cave?'

'Could be, Perry. Could be.' Macleod turned his attention back to Jona. 'Search that cave. Just make sure there isn't a ring in there. Or some other item of jewellery.'

'I will do, Seoras. Let me know what the item is you dig up.'

'Of course,' said Macleod, and closed down the call.

Perry was taking photographs around the room with his

mobile phone. He photographed the receipts as well, before putting them into a small envelope. Macleod had carefully used gloves when looking at them and searching the room, and he wondered if it was worth getting Jona to have a look at the room as well. Slowly, he made his way downstairs, where Sylvia and James were still sitting.

Alice had fallen asleep on the sofa, and had a blanket draped around her, the constable still sitting beside her.

'Did you find anything?' asked Sylvia.

'I just was going through some receipts,' said Macleod. 'I haven't got any answers for you now. I will try to find some answers for you. But that's all I can do. And then bring someone to justice. I can't bring him back. I'm so very sorry for your loss. I will do what I can. But I also can't promise anything.'

Sylvia nodded and curled up again while James stood up and went to shake Macleod's hand. 'I'm sure you'll do your best, Inspector.'

Macleod felt choked up as he shook the man's hand. He wanted out of that house as quick as possible. It didn't do for him to be emotional during the case. You had to be remote. You had to be away from it.

'And I will,' he said to the man. Stepping outside, Macleod got into the car, followed by Perry.

'Where to?' said Perry.

'Station. Sit down and think this through. Decent cup of coffee.'

Macleod heard the engine start, and the heat began to come slowly through the blower. Frozen, but the cold he was feeling wasn't from the outside air—it was the cold of seeing the shock and the absolute hopelessness a death left behind.

Chapter 11

'Coffee, sir?' said a voice.

Macleod was just taking his coat off. He hadn't warmed up yet, and he rubbed his hands together.

'Please, Ross, please. Have you come up with anything yet?'

'Not so far. What about yourself?'

'Found some receipts. The wine in the cave is Danny Poland's wine. Whether he went there first and then came back, or whatever, we don't know. Maybe he was being watched. We think he's definitely been with someone. There's also a note for the jewellers, a receipt. It's handwritten. I can't make it out, but it's not expensive. Fifty quid.'

'Seventeen-year-old kid,' said Ross. 'Expensive for a kid.'

'You go to a jewellers to buy an item that costs when it's something special. His parents said he was happy,' said Macleod.

'You think it was—'

'Yes, a girl. Well, I think it's a girl.'

'It could have been a boy.'

Macleod looked at Ross. 'Well, I think it's a girl. They said nothing about him being . . .'

'Gay,' said Ross.

'I still have trouble saying it,' said Macleod. 'You think that's a hangover? How does it not get easy to say it?'

'You were brought up with it, sir.'

'Does it not bother you,' said Macleod, 'that I can't get past it, that there seems to be something there that always makes me hesitate?'

'How you were brought up. If I had a problem with it, I wouldn't have made you godfather to my child.'

'I guess not,' said Macleod.

He smiled and watched Ross disappear off to make the coffee. It had been a strange number of years working with Ross and the rest of them. It had changed him. He hoped for the better.

Macleod sat down in his seat and waited for the coffee which Ross shortly put down in front of him. Perry shambled in not long after and stood beside one of the radiators in the room.

He didn't move from there for fifteen minutes. Macleod could see Ross was getting annoyed. The trouble Ross had with Perry, as Macleod saw it, was he didn't understand when Perry was working. Perry was working like mad as he stood at the radiator, warming his hands. Perry's real skill was the thinking. It wasn't searching.

Yes, he could do the detective work where you pulled out this and that and whatever, but his actual abilities were thinking and watching people. Perry read situations. He mulled over them, produced ideas and thoughts. Macleod knew he'd picked the right person for Hope, and he also knew that she never would have seen it. Perry wasn't the same as Macleod, but he was in a similar vein.

'What are you thinking?' Macleod asked him.

'Why Danny Poland? He's there with a girlfriend? Possibly. Why kill Danny Poland? What's Danny Poland got to do with anything?' said Perry. 'I don't think they wanted to kill Danny Poland.'

'What are you on about?' said Ross. 'Took off his clothing. They must have followed him at some point. They must have—'

'They didn't want to kill Danny Poland—not that they didn't want to kill that person— they didn't want to kill Danny Poland because Danny Poland's not part of the case. Our murderer wanted to kill somebody who was part of the case. They wanted to—'

There was a rap at the door. It opened and the young constable from the front office put her head in.

'Another phone call,' said Macleod.

'Yes,' she stopped for a moment, 'sir,' as if she'd just remembered the name, 'but it's not for you, it's for DC Perry. Warren Perry?'

Perry stepped away from the radiator and over to the door. 'The phone's out here, is it?'

'Yes,' she said.

'Back in a moment,' said Perry.

Perry followed the constable out to the front office and there picked up the phone. 'This is Detective Constable Warren Perry. Who am I speaking to?'

'This is Bic.'

'What's up?' asked Perry.

'I wanted to, um, ask,' he said. 'I just heard—'

'What have you heard?' asked Perry.

'Danny Poland. I mean, it's all around the school. It's all around everybody. Danny's dead.'

'Unfortunately, Danny Poland is dead. Was he a friend?'

'He was a mate,' said Bic. 'Decent mate.'

99

'What sort of a mate?' asked Perry.

'He went to the same school as us. Hung about together sometimes.'

'Would you have seen him regularly then?'

'Yeah, several times a week.'

'He ever go drinking with you, lads?'

'Yeah.'

'He ever been out to that cave or anything similar? Did he know about the cave?'

'Been told, but he didn't want to come out that night with us. He said that it was other things he wanted to do.'

'Did he say what?'

'No.'

'Are you okay?' asked Perry.

'Sure,' said the boy. But his voice didn't say that. His voice said something was wrong.

'Do the rest of your lads know?' asked Perry.

'Talking to them now on social media. I said I would call you to see what you knew.'

'Well, I can't tell you everything I know,' said Perry. 'But did you know what he was up to? What Danny was looking to do? Do you know if he was probably meeting someone?'

'We haven't seen Danny since we went off to the cave. That night, he said he couldn't be with us. I don't know what he was doing the nights after that.'

'Was Danny seeing a girl at all?'

'Danny? No.'

'Danny wasn't seeing a girl?'

'Don't think so.'

'Was he seeing a boy?' asked Perry.

'No. What are you saying? Danny's not gay. Danny's . . .

well, he's like us, you know.'

'Could Danny swim?'

'A bit. He wasn't a strong swimmer.'

'Could he use a boat? Had he any experience?' asked Perry.

'No. No,' said Bic. 'Danny disappeared off quite a bit without his parents knowing.'

'They hadn't reported him missing because he'd been gone nearly two nights then.'

'Well, sometimes Danny would come and stay at one of ours. Or we'd head out and camp somewhere.'

'So the trip out together, that wasn't unusual?'

'Oh, the trip to the cave was unusual. We'd done nothing like that. But sometimes if our parents were away, we'd crash at each other's. So there were plenty of times when we would be away from home,' said Bic.

'You'd buy booze and stuff, would you?'

'Yeah.'

'Did Danny mention anything about going to the jewellers in Thurso?'

'No,' said Bic. 'Don't know anything about that. Why? What's up with that? Has the jeweller had something to do with this?'

'The jeweller's got nothing to do with it. Don't go off making conclusions on things I've said when I haven't said anything,' said Perry. 'But a bit of advice. Don't go anywhere. Don't go off on your own at the moment, okay?'

'Why?' said Bic. 'Did somebody get to Danny? Why would somebody get to Danny? What's Danny got to do with any of this?'

'We're still working on it,' said Perry. 'But as soon as we know, we'll let you know. Anyway, get back to bed. Best you

101

try to get some sleep. I'm sorry for your loss. Sure it's a shock.'

'Yeah,' said Bic. He put the phone down.

Perry left the front office and made his way back to the little room the team were using. He marched back in and stood up against the radiator again, putting his hands down on it.

'Who was that?' asked Macleod.

It took Perry a moment before he looked up. 'Sorry,' said Perry. 'That was Bic. Apparently he knew Danny Poland. It seems they all knew Danny Poland. Danny used to drink with them, stayed over at some of theirs.'

'And?'

'Well, he knows nothing about Danny Poland with a girl, and he certainly wasn't with a boy, because he wasn't that way inclined,' said Perry.

'Well, he was with somebody,' said Macleod. 'You don't have an empty condom packet without someone around.'

'I said he didn't know he was with someone. But you know what it's like,' said Perry. 'If you've got a girl in mind, and depending on who that girl is, maybe you don't want your mates to be around when you see her. Maybe she's really special. Maybe Danny had a serious girl.'

'And he's going to the jewellers,' said Macleod. 'You think he could be?'

'Empty condom packet, to the jewellers. Is it their first time? Who knows? But I'm thinking that he got disturbed.'

'Did you put our constables out to watch over our four witnesses?'

'I did.'

'Have we had any disturbances?'

'Not been informed of any. Just told Bic to make sure he stays indoors.'

'I don't like this then,' said Macleod. 'If you're conjecturing that Danny Poland might have been killed by mistake—'

'Yes,' said Perry. 'You make one mistake, you can make another easily. We never released the names of the witnesses, did we?'

'Well, I can't,' said Macleod. 'They can't even be put on the telly. They're underage. I've got to keep their anonymity.'

'Of course,' said Perry. 'So, people will know that something has happened. Rumour will get out about how some lads found the body. So who are those lads? If you're a killer, did they think that the lads might have seen something? Did the lads—'

'You don't think the killer was quite close when they were in there? You don't think it wasn't that long before they actually . . .'

'Before they what?' asked Perry.

'Well, maybe the lads were so close timewise; maybe the killer was not long away before they arrived. Maybe they're worried that the boys actually saw something.'

'But what would tell them they saw something? The boys didn't see anything. They never reported anything. Anything that the boys saw when they were in the cave,' said Perry, 'was still there. Nothing removed.'

'No, but maybe somebody got spooked because we were with them so quickly. Maybe—'

'What you think,' said Perry, 'that the killer thinks we were put onto them by the boys.'

'Well, that would mean it would be one of the businesses. But we told everybody we were investigating purely because of the franchise links,' said Macleod. 'In which case—'

'In which case what?' said Ross, listening in.

'In which case, the killer must have thought that the boys

caught a glimpse of them. They wouldn't know what the boys did or didn't see. They didn't know that the body had gone out. If the body had slipped out beforehand. Problem is,' said Macleod, 'we don't know what the killer did, where they were, if they saw the boys or not. But if they thought the boys had some sort of evidence, they might come for them again.'

'I'll inform the constables. Stay with them for the next couple of days, put a rotating shift in, make sure the boys don't come out of the house,' said Perry.

'That's a very good idea,' said Macleod. 'Very good idea.' He looked down at his watch. 'Another hour or two, we'll be able to head off to the jewellers,' said Macleod. 'I'll be ready for breakfast soon; do you know that?'

'I was thinking about that, sir,' said Ross. 'They've got a little kitchen here. We could pop out to the supermarket and get some stuff.'

'You keep going with what you're doing. I need time to think,' said Macleod. He pulled out a scrap of paper. 'What do you want for breakfast, Ross?'

'You can't do that,' said Ross. 'I'll organise it; I'm—'

'Perry, give us a minute.'

Perry looked over at Macleod and gave a sigh as he moved himself off the radiator. 'Do you know where there's another good one of these?' he said as he left the room. As soon as he was away, Macleod made his way over and put his hands on the radiator.

'Alan,' said Macleod.

'What's the matter?' said Ross. 'You've called me Alan.'

'Yes I have, Alan. You're a sergeant now; you don't do the breakfasts; you don't run around like that.'

'With all due respect, you're the DCI and you're about to do it.'

'Yes, but that's because at the moment, I've got nothing to do. Nothing to do and I need to think. I won't be able to think in here because you'll interrupt and some of the rest of them will too. I'll also be able to drive in my car and put the heating on and get warm. So I will get the breakfast.'

'You need to be less thinking about what's going on in terms of logistics and get more into your head what's going on with the case. Hope will need you to help solve cases and not just because you dug through a computer. That's spade work. You're not paid to do spade work anymore. You're paid to do brain work.'

'I thought that was what Perry was for.'

'Perry gives you the conjecture. Perry gives you everything that makes you think why something is happening, but the brain work keeps it all together. I didn't become successful over these last couple of years because of what I did,' said Macleod. 'It's because of what we did, as a team.'

'But it's a different team now. And you're no longer in that role. I know you had problems when the kid came along. Struggled with the time away and that. But you got past those. But now you need to be there for Hope. Her wingman. Not a logistics manager. You need less time on the computer and more time in your head. Do you understand me?'

'Yes, sir.'

'And it's not 'sir.' Would you for once call me Seoras?' said Macleod.

'Yes, sir—call you Seoras.'

Macleod gave a wry grin, stood up off the radiator and said, 'Now would you give me your order or I'm coming back with a vegetarian breakfast for you.'

Chapter 12

Macleod left Perry at the station to continue his inquiries. Macleod, after cooking breakfast for everyone, made his way to the jewellers. He'd had time to think and ponder while he was doing the scrambled eggs, sausages, and bacon. He was feeling better, despite being up all night. It was something he got used to, that method of keeping going.

It didn't help with the cold, though. The more tired you were, the colder you felt, and Macleod could do with a couple of hours' sleep. However, by the time he got to Thurso, the small town was alive, despite the chill. He parked the car, walked round in his large coat and beanie hat to find the jewellers on the corner of one of the main streets.

As he entered the shop, a little bell rang and from behind the counter, a man appeared. As jeweller's shops went, it was the old kind. Cramped, but with lots and lots of rings and necklaces on show, all hidden away in glass cabinets.

'Good morning, sir,' said the man.

He looked round about Macleod's age, probably not far off retirement. He was dressed smartly in a waistcoat and trousers. There was even a pocket watch in his breast pocket. His hair was neatly trimmed, grey, and he gave a rather pleasant sparkle when he smiled towards Macleod.

'Looking for something for the missus?' he said, then he glanced down at Macleod.

'No, actually,' said Macleod. 'I'm here on business.'

'And what business would that be, sir?' asked the man.

'My name is Detective Chief Inspector Seoras Macleod. I'm currently investigating some deaths along the way.'

'Ah,' said the man. 'How can I help you with that? I'm not aware of having any involvement,' he whispered.

'Well, you probably won't be aware of it. However, a young lad died recently. And I believe he may have been in your shop.'

'Young lad?'

'Yes,' said Macleod.

He pulled out a small plastic bag which had the receipt in it, and placed it down on the counter in front of the man.

'Is this your handwriting?'

'It is. That's one of my receipts.'

'Do you not have one of those tills these days?'

'Don't have need of it, to be honest. I do take card payment and that, but I still do a handwritten receipt.'

'Can you tell me what the receipt says, sir?'

The man looked at Macleod. 'It's right there.'

'I'm afraid I can't read your handwriting,' said Macleod. 'Can you tell me what it says?'

'It's for a ring, black stone,' he said. 'Fairly inexpensive one, fifty pounds. It would look a bit like—' The man quickly moved across his shop and then delved into a glass cabinet. He brought a tray of rings up. 'One of these,' he said. 'That one there. It would look very similar to that.'

Macleod saw a gold ring with a black stone set on top.

'Not an expensive one, then?'

'No, the one I sold doesn't quite have the same sort of edging, but it's similar. I'd certainly be able to recognise it if I saw it again.'

'And you remember selling it?' asked Macleod.

'I do. It was a young lad and a young woman. Strange though.'

'In what way?' asked Macleod.

'Well, he came in first. I mean, didn't look like the sort of lad who would be in here. Don't get that many young lads in here at all, if I'm truthful. More gentlemen like yourself or our wives coming in looking. It'd be watch straps, things like that. So, in truth, I don't usually get anybody of that age in.'

'And what was he looking for?'

'Engagement ring. I showed him some further up, but I could tell by the look on his face, they were a little out of his budget. Actually, they were a long way out of his budget. So, I showed him these. They're not exactly engagement rings, but, you know, what's an engagement ring? Could be anything,' said the man. 'And then a girl came in.'

'Can you describe her?' asked Macleod.

'Well, she had long, blonde hair. Quite thin legs. Very . . . I don't know. How would you put it? She was thin. Not unattractive, but thin, I think beneath the coat she was wearing. It was a big coat. She had her hood up, but you could see the blonde hair hanging out. She took the hood down at one point. The hair looked long, wavy, more of a dirty blonde than a straight blonde,' said the man.

'What age would you say she was?'

The man looked at him. 'I have no idea,' he said. 'Can't tell when I look at them. You look at them and they could be thirteen, they could be twenty-three. I am clueless.'

'And the boy, what age would you say he was?'

'Fifteen, nineteen, I don't know,' said the man.

'Well, he was seventeen. Would you say she looked older or younger?'

'Maybe, maybe younger, but not by a lot. She could have been older, of course, I don't know.'

'But she was wearing what?'

'A big blue coat,' said the man. 'Black leggings, they call them. I find them quite funny because they look to me like stuff you'd wear in the gym but they all seem to wear them everywhere.'

'Did she undo the coat at all? Did you see what she was wearing underneath?'

The man shook his head. 'That's part of the problem. I can't describe the rest of her figure. But the legs were thin and I don't think it was just the tightness of the leggings. She had boots on. Black boots.'

'What about her face?' asked Macleod.

'Quite a small mouth and a thin nose.'

'Do you notice anything else about her?'

'She was nervous, and I don't think she was nervous because of him. She came in rather sheepishly and didn't look at me.'

'So what happened when she came in?'

'Well, I'd held the ring out to the lad, and he turned round and he showed it to her. She gave a nod and then she gave him a hug and a kiss. Nothing ridiculous, just a quick one. And then she disappeared, leaving him to pay for it.'

'She didn't take it with her then?'

'No, he took it. I was going to give him a box for it, but he said no and dropped it into one of these little parcel bags. Here, one of these.' The man put a little bag out on the table. It was barely bigger than your thumb.

'How did he pay?'

'Cash. That's why I gave him that receipt. I said to him that if in the next week if things didn't work out, he was welcome to give me it back and I'd give him his fifty pounds back. He kind of looked at me, and I just said to him, you know, I know how these things go. She looked nervous, so if it doesn't work out for you, I said, I'll take it back. He gave me a smile, actually. Said it was pretty decent. It's about the best I get from the young people these days.' The man gave a smile, and then he frowned. 'This is the young lad they found in the water, is it?'

'I'm afraid so, sir. It's important if you can remember anything they said to each other.'

'She came in,' the man said. 'She didn't say anything. But then I left him to look at the ring and I went to the far end of the shop. I'm not that far away. And they were whispering. But I did overhear, he said to her, that it was all arranged for that night. They talked about one day getting their own place. But they were going to seal it that night.'

'What do you think they meant by that?' asked Macleod.

'I don't know,' said the man. 'They had a ring. What are they going to do with the ring? Were they going to run off and get married? Were they going to, well, consummate? That was the old term, wasn't it?'

'It was indeed,' said Macleod. 'In the old days, you didn't consummate until you were married.'

'Well, that's what they told you,' said the shopkeeper. 'I think a lot of consummation was done before you were married.'

Macleod probably had to admit to himself that he may have been right.

'If I remember right,' said Macleod, 'you said he came in first, she then comes in, they have a small chat, she goes, he goes?'

'That's about the long and the short of it. I remember it well because it was quite a sweet moment. You don't see them that young coming in.'

'And the way they were with each other, would you say?'

'He was besotted with her. Absolutely. The eyes lit up when she came in.'

'You didn't get a name, did you?' asked Macleod.

'No, I didn't,' he said. 'I'd recognise her again, if you can give me a photo or whatever. Description is about the best I can do.'

'Fair enough,' said Macleod. He reached over with his hand and shook the man's hand. 'If I need to get a hold of you again, are you going away anywhere soon?'

'No,' said the man. 'I'll be about. You can phone the shop. Or do you want my mobile number?'

'I know where you are,' said Macleod. 'That's fair enough. Here,' he said, and handed one of his cards over. 'If anything else comes to mind you think might be useful, or you remember anything else about your encounter here with the pair of them, call me, let me know.'

'Poor girl,' said the man. 'Do you think she knows?'

'I don't know who she is, so that's kind of an impossible question to answer,' said Macleod. 'And if I could, I'm afraid I can't.'

'Yes. Sorry,' said the man. 'Probably a bit of a daft statement.'

'Thank you for your help though,' said Macleod. 'It's been very useful.'

He left the jewellers back out into the cold. There was now hail coming down and quickly he raced to the car, getting inside, switching it on but just sitting there allowing the heat to build within it. He needed to get hold of the local constables. He needed them to do a scan round the school. Was anybody missing? Was anybody not there? Was anyone acting strangely? However, it was Saturday. And being Saturday, the school wouldn't be in. So there wouldn't be anyone to find out about. Macleod had his hand on the wheel. That was annoying.

Macleod pulled away in the car, heading back to the station. In his mind, he was building up a picture of what had gone on. Somebody had killed Stephen Ludlow. So far, Macleod didn't know why. The man was setting up franchises. Had he offended some of them? Had he been caught out? After all, he'd had sex with Gail Harmon. Had she killed him? Had he done something beyond what he should have done? But then, why would she have admitted to having sex? Had he offended the Achterbergs? Was Carmen angry at how he had lusted after Selina?

Had Tabitha found out something? Clearly, the man wasn't averse to playing away from home. What was their relationship like, anyway? Was there something wrong with the work? Was there a chance for somebody to get rid of him? Or was there something further back in his history or out of the area that caused somebody to come to kill him? Macleod thought that the long-distance idea was becoming less likely.

Danny Poland, what had happened to him? Was there an angle here that they didn't know about Danny Poland? Seemingly, he'd been off to have a night with his girlfriend. And a special night, by the sounds of it. Had they seen something? Had they watched the killer in action? But then again, that had been nights before.

Or was the killer making a mistake? Danny was part of the

group, wasn't he? Perry had said that in the conversation, that Danny had hung out with the boys. But he hadn't been with them. That made Macleod think it could be somebody from the local area. Somebody who had seen them about. That happened when you lived there. You started to see familiar figures.

Maybe they had just associated it. Had they only seen one of the boys? Had they seen the boys at all? Danny Poland had been an unfortunate victim of a lack of knowledge of a killer. He just didn't know who had seen him.

But where was Danny Poland's girlfriend? Who was it? She could be in danger at the moment, thought Macleod. They would need to find her, and quick.

He'd also have to think more about the witnesses. The four lads could be a way in for him to find the killer. Surely by now, the killer would have realised that there were constables staying at the house. Unwittingly, Macleod might have given the killer an opportunity to identify them properly. One thing about up here was the villages were quite spread out.

The killer hadn't seen the different houses at the time. Maybe they'd run on instinct. Maybe as the killer, they didn't want to be seen anywhere near the houses. After all, they killed Danny when he was away from his.

Who wanted Ludlow dead? thought Macleod. *So far we don't know. So far, we only have hypotheses, most of them not substantiated. He played about, but had he been caught? Had he been offending someone with his sexual activities?*

Macleod sighed. *It would not get any warmer either, would it? Station, coffee, witnesses. Perry seemed to have a rapport with the boys. I might bring him with me.* Macleod was already planning his day.

Chapter 13

Macleod stood in front of the filter coffee machine with his right hand sitting on the glass carafe. It had been put on some twenty minutes earlier but only now had he reached it. He had a cup off to one side but he continued to stand holding on to the carafe. In front of him was a notice about kitchen rules and where the cutlery should go. But his eyes, although they looked at it, weren't reading it.

'I know we all like our coffee,' said Perry, 'but I didn't realise there was an exact moment when you had to pour it.'

Macleod turned to Perry and gave a wry smile. 'Don't complain. Pouring my own now.'

'You poured your own down in Glasgow?'

'I know. It was instant down there. Developed quite a habit for the good stuff up here. And you no longer smoke,' said Macleod, smiling.

'I guess we've both improved, then. Well, apparently not enough,' said Perry.

'What do you mean?' asked Macleod.

'Still single,' said Perry. 'And the last time I checked my calendar, there aren't a lot of dates in there for me to go on.'

'If you're looking for advice about women and dating,' said

Macleod, 'really don't talk to me. You'll have much better luck with Ross than me.'

Perry laughed at that. Macleod turned back again, staring at the sign about the cutlery.

'I don't find the cutlery that difficult,' said Perry.

'What?' said Macleod, suddenly.

'The cutlery,' said Perry, pointing at the sign. 'I've nailed it. It's not a problem to me.'

'I'm thinking,' said Macleod.

'I did get that,' said Perry.

'We should talk to our witnesses again.'

'Yes,' said Perry. 'They called in. I think they know Danny. Probably know him well.'

'I believe so. He also was off doing something on his own, Danny Poland. I'm wondering if . . . maybe,' said Macleod suddenly and then stopped.

'What?' said Perry.

'Ross will tell me off. Suppositions. Well, the killer, I think he's gone after Danny Poland because he thinks the boys saw something. But, of course, Danny Poland wasn't there. So, our killer doesn't know who.'

'But he must know some of them,' said Perry. 'To know Danny was part of the group.'

'Probably,' said Macleod. 'Or he knows of them. Or an idea about them. Or he's got rumours of them. I take it their parents are all aware?' said Macleod.

'I said to them, but, well, you know what parents are like. Some of them jumped all over it. One or two of them just seemed angry at the boys, annoyed at what they got involved in.'

'Let's go see them.'

115

'Where do you want to go first?' said Perry. 'Which one?'

'Let's go talk to Lorry. He's the youngest, isn't he?'

'He was the one that was puking,' said Perry. 'Hopefully, he's stopped that by now.'

Macleod took the carafe, pouring coffee into his cup. Perry put a flask down beside him of the tall variety that you take with you on picnics.

'What's that?' asked Macleod.

'In case we get any midnight callouts again. Don't like you not having any coffee. You look like me without a cigarette.'

'Well, I'm not giving you a load of cigars to take with you,' said Macleod.

'I wouldn't smoke them anyway,' said Perry.

'I'll tie up with Ross,' said Macleod, 'and we'll head out in ten minutes, okay? Make sure you've got the addresses. I never remember them.'

Perry nodded and left. Macleod remembered what Ross did. He always provided addresses. He always had all the details for the case. *Should he be taking his sergeant with him?* When he re-entered from the kitchen into the small room that they were working out of, Ross was busy behind his computer.

Macleod could make Ross come with him, because realistically, wasn't that where he should be? He seemed to migrate to the computer all the time. He was good at it but Hope should bring him out. Macleod stopped. This was Hope's team. Either Ross did it and came out and asked to be with Macleod, or Hope would have to put him in whatever place she wanted him. He couldn't do everything for her. He wandered over to Ross and explained that he and Perry were off to see the young witnesses again.

'Looking up the past history of Stephen Ludlow. I'll let you know if I've got something new.'

'Okay,' said Macleod, almost sighing.

He turned and picked up the flask he'd previously filled and took it with him out to the car where Perry awaited. Twenty minutes later, they were walking up to the house of the child known as Lorry. It was on an estate. Before he got up to the door, Macleod could see the constable from inside approaching the front door to open it.

'Morning, sir,' said the young constable.

'Inspector will do,' said Macleod, 'if we're in front of others. Otherwise, it's Seoras, as you are . . . ?'

'Daniel. Daniel Taggart.'

'Constable Taggart. Lead us in. Everything okay?'

'Have seen no one come to the house. And we had a quiet night, as far as I can tell.'

'Good. Keep your eyes peeled. With the demise of Danny Poland, it gives me great concern for these witnesses.'

'Course, Inspector.'

As Macleod was about to enter what he thought would be the living room, the door opened, and a short five-foot woman stared up at him.

'Is my Kyle safe?' she thundered. Kyle was Lorry's real name.

'I take it you're Kyle's mother,' said Macleod.

'You're damn right I am. Is he safe?'

'Can we sit down for a moment?' said Macleod. 'We need to talk about this sensibly, quietly, so you understand.'

'That's not what I asked you. I—'

'I left Constable Taggart with you,' said Macleod. 'He reports a quiet night. He also said they've had no other issues at the moment.'

'That's not what Kyle's saying.'

'Well, then let's talk to Kyle,' said Macleod. He half-ushered the woman into the living room, where she turned and took a seat beside the young man, occasionally known as Lorry. Macleod sat down in a seat while Perry stood beside him.

Lorry looked up at Perry, giving him half a smile.

'Morning, Lorry,' said Perry. 'You okay, son?'

'I think so. The other lads are . . . well—'

'What?' asked Macleod.

'Go on; tell him. Tell him,' said his mum.

'Well, I've been talking to Jimbo and Cheeks and Bic. They reckon they've seen cars outside they don't recognise.'

'One particular one?' asked Macleod. 'Or many different ones?'

'They're saying lots of different ones. Not sure. Certainly, they haven't said the same car. But also, Bic went out shopping with his folks. Thought somebody was following him. Jimbo said that too.'

'They haven't mentioned it to us.'

'Well, it depends, doesn't it? Jimbo's dad doesn't want any trouble. What with his, well, previous convictions.'

Macleod raised an eyebrow. 'Previous convictions?'

'Jimbo's mother's left. His dad's here. So, Jimbo lives with him now, but Jimbo really has to look after himself,' said Lorry.

'That's interesting,' said Macleod. 'You haven't been out, though?'

'He's not going out of this house until I know he's safe. Can you tell me, is he safe?' spat Kyle's mum.

'At the moment,' said Macleod, 'I think it is best if Kyle stays in the house. We'll see about Monday in school. If we haven't found the killer of Danny Poland, what we might do is station some officers in the school. To be honest, any adult will stand

118

out amongst the staff. They shouldn't be there. But we'll cross that bridge closer to the school day. We'll need to talk to the head about that as well. But, in the meantime, I think you should keep Kyle here in the house. I'll keep Constable Taggart, or one of his colleagues, with you too.'

'If we see anything?' asked Kyle.

'Then you call us, Lorry,' said Perry. He walked over, crouched down beside Lorry, looking up into his eyes. 'You're going to be okay. You saw something that was nasty. It's pulled you into a situation. But we're going to look after you, okay? That's why Constable Taggart's here. He's a good man, as are his colleagues. We know what's gone on. We know someone's been murdered. It's not somebody approaching you from anywhere that you don't know about, or we don't know about. Leave it to us, the Detective Chief Inspector. He'll find who's behind this.'

'Are you that one off the telly?' said Lorry suddenly.

Macleod gave a quizzical look.

'He sees you on the telly,' said Kyle's mum. 'We've all seen you on the telly. You've got that hat and coat.'

'I do a lot of the statements to the press, being a detective chief inspector.'

The telephone of the house rang and Kyle's mother stood up, excusing herself, and went off to answer it. When she left the room, Kyle glanced over at Perry and then back at Macleod.

'You usually work with that other woman, don't you?' said Kyle.

'Which other woman? I have several women on my team,' said Macleod.

'Somebody said she used to do the press, but she doesn't anymore. She's tall, got red hair.'

'That's Detective Inspector Hope McGrath.'

'Is she coming up?' asked Lorry.

'She's on holiday at the moment,' said Macleod, not wishing to say any more. 'Why do you ask?'

'Jimbo was asking.'

Macleod stared at Lorry for a moment. 'Why would Jimbo need to know if Inspector McGrath was coming?'

'Well, well . . . he . . .'

Perry began to laugh.

'What?' Macleod looked over.

'What did Jimbo say?' asked Perry.

There was a cheeky grin springing across Lorry's face. 'I can't tell you, I can't tell you. If my mother heard, she'll not be happy.'

'Some boy's crush,' said Perry. 'You can tell us.'

Lorry blushed for a moment and then said, 'Jimbo fancies her rotten. Says she's got a cracking arse on her. He likes a redhead.'

Macleod's face went sombre, but Perry burst out laughing.

'I would advise Jimbo,' said Macleod, 'that he doesn't speak about her in that way if she's around. Stay in the house,' said Macleod. 'We'll be in touch.'

He went to exit out of the room but saw Perry looking back at Lorry and smiling. As he entered the hallway, Kyle's mother came back off the phone.

'It's just his aunt calling,' she said. 'Are you off?'

'It seems okay here. I feel as if I'm seeing things in the dark. I need to talk to others,' said Macleod. 'The constable will stay, and whatever happens, tell him straight away. He'll pass anything suspicious to us. We'll look after your boy as best we can.'

'Just find whoever's after him.'

'If indeed there is somebody after him,' said Macleod.

They stepped outside of the house, into the car, and as Perry turned on the engine, Macleod turned to him.

'There was no need to encourage the boy. Hope struggles as it is. You know she's had to work hard to get people to see her as a detective, and not just some sort of force pin-up. Senior officers don't help in that,' said Macleod, almost spitting.

'He's a teenage boy. They're teenage boys. Hope's heading towards her thirties. The older woman that looks superb,' said Perry, 'is perfectly natural. And yes, he shouldn't say it in front of her, should keep it to himself. But you can't blame a boy for growing up.'

Macleod thought back to his own childhood. He didn't speak things like that out in society. But yes, some men would speak like that, but never his father. His father had been serious, very serious. If he'd have caught Macleod speaking like that, well, maybe that was the problem, Macleod wondered. He hadn't been allowed to talk like that. He hadn't had many friends to share that side of things with. Would they have called it repression these days? He didn't know.

Perry spun the car out of the drive and looked down to find the next address. As he did so, Macleod's phone vibrated. He picked it up and put it to his ear. 'Hello, it's Inspector Macleod.'

'Inspector, it's Constable Barnes at the station. Just had a phone call. The boy Jimbo has called in. Says he's seen a female stalker. He says he's on his own.'

Macleod looked across at Perry. 'Jimbo, where's Jimbo's house?'

'A place called Bighouse, near Melvich.'

'Go,' said Macleod. 'Go!'

121

Perry put his foot to the floor and the car raced off. As it did so, a shard of hail hit the car from the clouds above. It was only halfway through the morning, but everywhere looked dark and Perry fought to see the road, the wipers struggling to clear away the hail that was driving into the windscreen.

'Best speed, Perry,' said Macleod. 'We're not losing another one.'

Chapter 14

Bighouse was more a small collection of houses rather than a village, and Perry drove quickly towards the house closest to the coast. Jimbo and his father occupied a rather run-down affair, and through the driving hail, Macleod could see a figure emerging at the far end of it. The clouds had rolled in and the wind was howling. There must have been some sort of storm cloud above, and the figures ahead were not truly distinct.

'I'm not sure how much further the car is going to go once we reach the house. They look like they're going across the field,' said Perry.

'Take it as far as you can.'

Macleod was prepared, wrapped up in his coat, with his fedora hat firmly placed on his head. He had a scarf around his neck, whereas Perry simply had his suit jacket. Macleod understood. Perry didn't enjoy driving in a large coat. But it would also mean the man would get battered as soon as he got out of the car.

The car dipped suddenly, hitting a large pothole. Perry fought with the wheel. The back end spun slightly, and then they arrived at the house. The figures were beyond it; two figures, one racing after the other. Macleod presumed it was Jimbo up ahead, but the one behind him, as far as he could tell, was not that tall.

Perry suddenly slammed on the brakes and the car came to a grinding halt in front of a fence.

'That's it,' said Perry. Macleod was out of the car before Perry, got to the fence, and clambered over. Beside him, Perry jumped. Macleod struggled to see ahead, the hailstorm continuing. He had to put a hand up to shield his eyes as the tiny shards of compact ice tore into them, sweeping in from the coast.

'Hard as you can, Perry, hard as we can,' said Macleod. He felt the squelch of his shoes, glad he had his lace-ups on rather than his slip-ons, which probably would have come off. Macleod's shoes were of good quality, and he could spend all day on his feet.

The ground was damp, and as he ran, he went through a sludgy patch. He felt himself skid for a moment, put his hands out, and barely kept his balance. However, he pushed on again. Behind him, he heard Perry stumble. The larger man hit the ground, but Macleod didn't wait, instead continuing to run as best he could.

As Macleod looked ahead, he could see the sea beyond him. It wouldn't be that far to the cliffs. And indeed, Jimbo looked like he was reaching them.

'Cut right, you fool!' muttered Macleod under his breath. On the left-hand side was an inlet that ran down, producing a wide, almost sea-loch. To the right, the cliffs ran as far as the eye could see. If Jimbo had cut right, he would have stayed on the land, stayed easily within sight. But instead, the boy went over the edge. Macleod's heart skipped a beat for a moment.

Surely, he must have known a way down. He wouldn't have just jumped. Macleod saw the other figure, a short distance behind Jimbo. It wasn't letting up though, running smoother than Macleod was. It too, disappeared over the edge. Macleod cast a glance back and saw Perry fighting in sodden trousers.

'Too many blasted fags in the past, Perry,' said Macleod, as he turned and continued into the hailstorm. As he reached the coast, Macleod's fedora blew off. He felt the bracing wind whip through his hair. He almost skidded to a halt, seeing rocks falling away before him. The path was steep, if indeed it was a path, for it just looked like a collection of jagged rock.

He could see Jimbo below him, somewhere further down, and another figure. Was it female? It was female, wasn't it? It was slight enough to be female. He tried not to concentrate on the figure, but looked at the rocks beneath him. He needed to hurry, but one false step here and he could take a tumble, a tumble that could hurt badly or land him in the sea.

'This is the police!' shouted Macleod as loud as he could over the wind. 'Stop! This is the police. You've nowhere to go!'

He saw Jimbo look back up at him and knew that his voice must have carried, but the pursuing figure didn't look back. Instead, it began clambering down rocks.

Macleod made a jump, and stumbled falling forward. He threw his hands out and stopped his chin from driving into a rock, but his side hit hard. Macleod took a deep breath. He didn't feel like something was broken but it was a hard bang.

He swung his feet down, found his footing again, and continued clambering down the rocks. Macleod wanted to shout more, but he was winded from the fall. His hands were chilled. He had no gloves on, not having time to put them on as he had raced from the car. He wished he had now, because they were going numb.

As he clambered down the rock, he saw Jimbo was running out of rock to go to. The formation of the cliff had allowed for a path down towards the sea. But once you got right down towards the bottom, there was nowhere to go, the cliff too sheer to climb up or down. You'd have to retrace your steps. But tracing those steps was a pursuer, and Jimbo was now looking frightened.

He wasn't a small lad, not by any stretch of the imagination, but the figure ahead was coming forward relentlessly. As Macleod clambered on down the rock, he noted there was no hair on the figure.

Was it wearing a balaclava, a beanie? Was the hair tied up inside? Had he been correct in thinking it a woman? A woman with short hair?

He thought about those involved in the case. None of them had short hair. None of them were bald. The closest to bald would have been Mr Achterberg, but the figure was far too slender for him.

Macleod heard a noise behind him and some swearing. He glanced back to see Perry attempting to follow him down the rocks. The man must have been frozen, the jacket swinging open in the wind with just a shirt underneath.

Macleod continued his own descent, desperate to get down as quick as possible. Jimbo was in trouble. Macleod reached a point where he didn't think he could reach across. He would have to jump. The gap was there, and they all must have jumped it. And so he leapt, believing it better to go for it than to stand and think.

His foot landed on the other side. He skidded, stretching

out with both hands. His fingers, numb as they were, clung for all he was worth. He was there on the other side—just about. He turned and looked down.

The figure was only six or seven feet now from Jimbo. *Did they have a weapon?* Macleod was at least fifty feet away and so continued his descent, stumbling down, coming now to a part with the occasional loose rock. If he got this wrong, he'd be into the surf. The storm up above was throwing its fury down the cliff—was also whipping up the tide. Macleod felt himself get gently splashed. Further down towards Jimbo, the waves were crashing properly. They would sweep you away if you weren't careful.

Macleod couldn't think like that. He had to keep going, had to get down there. As he continued his descent, something in the back of his mind said to him: *Why isn't Hope here? This is why you need the top job. This is why you need to be out of this. You can't do this anymore. Hope would have gone down here like a whippet. Kirsten would have gone down here even quicker. Maybe even Susan. Ross could get down with a bit of alacrity. But no, Jimbo was lucky enough to receive Perry and me.*

Macleod was now thirty feet away and turned and clung onto the rock as a large wave hit. It threw its water up the rocks, landed on Macleod, but also Jimbo and his attacker. Macleod saw the attacker slip and tried to get back up onto their feet. As Macleod strode along, his feet slipped, the rocks now incredibly wet.

The attacker had leapt for Jimbo, grabbing hold of him. She pushed him into the rocks. Macleod, now only a few feet away, could see the balaclava on the head and the tight get-up around her. Dark blue bottoms with a tight blue fleece. Whoever she was, she was choking Jimbo with thick gloves.

Macleod got close and drove two hands into the back of the attacker. An elbow was flung up at him, striking him on the cheek, causing him to spin. He tumbled to the rocks, lying prone beside the attacker. She didn't move for him, but continued to throttle Jimbo. Macleod kicked hard at her ankles.

'I'm coming!' said a breathless Perry. 'I'm coming!'

Macleod had no idea where Perry was. Instead, he kicked at the ankles of the female. It had the desired effect as she turned towards him. Through the hail, he could barely make out the balaclava, never mind the eyes. There was nothing else to see.

She stepped forward, and he kicked hard at the knee, momentarily stopping her. Macleod was not a fighter, but you didn't spend as long in the job as he had without learning how to fight dirty. However, the person was on to him quickly, and his next kick was sidestepped.

She came down and drove a punch hard into his stomach. Macleod felt like he should retch, and he struggled to move, the wind knocked out of him. His attacker turned back to Jimbo, who had stood up now, clutching his throat. Macleod saw Jimbo's hand reach for the balaclava, trying to pull it off. But instead, Jimbo was grabbed and pulled in towards the attacker. It looked like she was going to snap his neck, twisting him, to come in behind him, an arm flung round his neck.

Macleod couldn't reach, and then over the top of him he saw what looked like a giant shadow. It was, in fact, Perry throwing himself at the attacker. Perry clattered into her back, sending him, the attacker, and Jimbo all onto the rocks. Perry cried out in pain but the attacker tumbled off to one side, landing on a rock ledge further down.

'Get on top of Jimbo! Get on top of him!' shouted Macleod

as another wave hit. It crashed high, dowsing them all, and Macleod saw Perry reach out, grabbing hold of Jimbo. The boy was sliding on the rock, and Macleod desperately pulled himself up and flung himself, grabbing hold of Jimbo's other leg. Macleod looked down.

There was no one on the rocks below. Desperately, Macleod scrabbled to his feet, looking here and there, waiting for the attack to come. But there was nothing. No one was scrabbling up the rocks. No one else was on that cliff face except Macleod, Perry, and Jimbo. Macleod felt the cold of the wind.

'Where'd she go?' gasped Perry. 'Where'd she go?'

'Are you all right?' said Macleod to Jimbo. 'Are you okay? Can you move?'

'I think so, I think so,' came Jimbo's gasping reply.

'Perry, we've got to get out of here. Those waves will take us down.'

'But where did she go?'

Macleod looked out to the sea. It couldn't be. There, among the waves, someone was swimming. Someone was strong enough to keep moving. Macleod went to reach for his phone. If he could get people moving here, if he could get the attacker, they could catch the killer. His hand went into his pocket. His mobile wasn't there.

'Perry, phone,' said Macleod. Perry was gasping.

'Car,' said Perry. 'Still in the car.'

'What's it doing in the car?'

'Charging,' said Perry. 'Bloody charging.'

'Grab Jimbo. We need to get back up. We need to get back up.'

'Where's your phone?' said Perry.

'It dropped out,' said Macleod.

Quickly, Macleod ushered Perry and Jimbo back up some rocks, and they climbed until they were clear of the crashing waves that were coming in. From there, they made their way more slowly up the cliff edge. They had to retreat across some gaps that they had jumped before. It was more awkward, but with three of them, and with no pursuer to think about, they made the arduous climb.

As they neared the top, Macleod could see police cars in the distance. There, also, was his phone. He picked it up, called Susan Cunningham, and told her to get things underway. He wanted the helicopter out; he wanted the lifeboat out. They needed to search for that killer. By the time Macleod had walked back to the car, an ambulance had arrived. Perry, Jimbo, and he were ushered into the back.

Perry's teeth were chattering, and he was wrapped in a foil blanket. Macleod picked up his phone, struggling to push the numbers, and called Susan Cunningham again.

'It's underway. Ross should come out to you,' said Susan. 'I have to go.'

The paramedic told Macleod to sit there while he checked his vitals. Macleod was cold, but not that cold. He didn't feel like he was endangered; he just needed warmed up. Jimbo, on the other hand, was going to make a trip to hospital.

About half an hour later, Macleod had got back to his hotel room to have a shower. Perry had been checked out as well—he was bruised and banged up, but nothing was broken, nothing that wouldn't heal up. Meanwhile, Susan Cunningham had got another search party out. As Macleod got out of the shower, he had a knock on his hotel room door. He looked through the peephole, saw Ross, opened it up, and allowed him into his room.

'Are you okay, sir?' asked Ross.

'I'm pretty banged up, Alan,' said Macleod. 'I'm not fit for that sort of thing these days.'

'No, sir. And Perry?'

'We're going to be okay. How's the boy?'

'Doctor says the boy will be fine. They're keeping him in, so I put a couple of constables on him to keep him company. Found his father as well.'

'What's the man doing leaving him?'

'The man was as drunk as anything, down at the local pub. Informed social services,' said Ross.

'Great. It's a woman we're looking for. It was a woman we were chasing. Susan find anything?'

'No, not so far, but we haven't been going that long,' said Ross. 'Did you say that she was swimming away?'

'Yes, swimming.'

'Swimming well?'

'How can you swim well in that stuff, Ross? It was crashing in, but she was making some sort of progress. I think she was making for a different place to get out.'

'We'll see if we can get her. At least you're okay.'

'Yes, Ross. I'm okay,' said Macleod. 'I'll meet you back at the station. Thanks for checking in.'

Ross left his room and Macleod, wrapped up in a dressing gown, went over to the window and stared out across Thurso. He picked up his phone and called Jane. This was different. Normally, Macleod could keep going forever in a case, but he needed to hear Jane's voice. He needed to take time out. For once, his first thought wasn't about the case. It was about how close he'd come to finding himself in real trouble.

Chapter 15

Susan Cunningham sighed and adjusted her prosthetic leg. It was better than hopping around on crutches—that was for sure. But every now and again, it just felt that bit sore. They said it was to do with settling in, getting used to walking on it. She thought that when it arrived, she'd want it on all the time, never wanting to take it off, because it would be like having her real leg back again.

Except it wasn't. It was useful, more than useful. It was enabling her to get about and to look normal. People stopped gazing at the space beneath her leg, looking at the crutches and pitying her.

Often, it took people some time to identify. She'd taken to wearing trousers that went all the way down and round about the ankle. And if you weren't looking carefully, you didn't see the metal pole that went into the foot.

One thing she was glad of was that Macleod was treating her no differently. She knew on the team, Perry and she would usually be assigned off to do the more menial tasks. Liaison, especially with a search team.

Susan knew that Macleod wouldn't be involved with looking over it. Search teams had an entire array of people who did search and did it well. Susan was just a liaison, feeding in potential information, relaying back to Macleod what had happened. But he left her to get on with it and expected it done well. He was not cutting her any slack because of the leg. And that made her happy. However, this had been a busy one. Searches conducted almost constantly, if not for the same people, over the last few days.

On top of that, Macleod had also tasked her with liaison with the varied restaurants that Ludlow had met the potential franchisees in. Between running back and forth, it had taken a bit of time tracking down who the restaurant owners were and interviewing the staff within. Many of them weren't there when Susan wanted them.

But she finally reckoned she had an accurate picture of all the visits. Macleod had said he was returning to the station after recovering at his hotel room. No sign of the would-be attacker had been found. She could be at the bottom of the sea, but the search advisor did say there was potential she could have gone to rocks and away.

It takes time to set up searches, time to get people into position, for lifeboats to be deployed and get to the area that was requiring to be searched. There was time for the woman to swim ashore and get away. The coastline of the north of Scotland was remote, not overly populated. So far, no one had reported a dripping wet woman in a balaclava.

Susan marched to the room at the station the team were occupying, and as she entered, she saw Macleod sitting in his chair, generally looking at nothing. She knew better than to turn round and annoy him when he was thinking and so made straight for the coffee filter machine, pouring herself one. She looked over her shoulder and saw him looking up, smiling.

'I'll get you one,' she said.

'Thank you. Ross, you want to come over for this? Susan's debrief.'

Ross came out from behind his computer, pulled a chair over beside Macleod's desk.

'I suppose you want one as well.'

'Well . . .'

'That's your direct boss,' said Macleod. 'You shouldn't have to ask. You should know how he likes his coffee, too.'

'He usually doesn't let me make it. I'm only pouring this, not making it.'

Macleod looked over at Ross, but the man was deliberately looking away. If anyone was going to make Macleod coffee, it would be Ross, because he'd make it right.

'So what did you find out?' said Perry, entering the room. Susan poured a fourth cup, and the team gathered around Macleod's desk.

'Well, I've been to all the restaurants. That Ludlow's some character.'

'In what way?' asked Macleod.

'Well, the last meeting with Carmen and Selina for example. I think you're aware, Carmen wasn't there the whole time, but she came at the end. According to the owner, Ludlow, and Selina were hitting it off rather well. He said that he thought there was chemistry happening. He was quite surprised when the other woman turned up.'

'Really?'

'Very much. The thing was, Selina was well dressed. "Like a woman on the prowl" was his description.'

'Right,' said Perry.

'And he said that Ludlow was all over her. However, when

Carmen arrived, she too was "dressed to kill", as he put it. Only, he didn't get the idea that she was interested in Ludlow.'

'So, what happened?' asked Perry.

'Well, he said that Carmen went to sit beside Selina, but she was only talking to Ludlow. Selina was ignoring Carmen, almost. He said he thought Carmen was trying to get her attention. But generally, she looked rather sullen, almost as if she'd been spurned.'

'Is this just the owner's impression?' asked Macleod. 'I take it he was male?'

'He was, but I talked to one waitress and she said he was right. It wasn't just a male eye on a female.'

'I think our Carmen likes Selina, a bit more than Selina likes Carmen,' said Perry.

'Even I'm picking that up,' said Ross.

'Was it a strong enough motive to get rid of Ludlow? I mean, as I understand this franchise business,' said Macleod, 'they'd set up the franchise and basically Ludlow would clear off. He wouldn't be around. He wouldn't be a long-term threat, would he?'

'Don't need to be a long-term threat,' said Susan. 'If she was that keen on Selina, maybe he was just a threat. You wouldn't want Jane nipping off for a quick one with another man, would you?'

Macleod was rather taken aback. 'Not that I think she would,' Susan added quickly.

'Well, I'm glad you've got that opinion of my partner,' said Macleod.

'She's right, though,' said Perry. 'You might not view it in your way, sir. When you look at Jane, you know that Jane's probably going to be around. She's in it for the long haul. So, it would have to be somebody who, in the long haul would take her away. Maybe Carmen doesn't think Selina will be here for the long haul. Maybe it is just a business partnership even though she wants more.'

'We're not that different,' said Ross. 'We can be as fickle.'

'I don't think anybody was suggesting you couldn't be, or you were that different,' said Macleod. He shifted uneasily, always bothered when same-sex-relationship talk came up. He still struggled with it, even though he was no longer against it.

'One thing about Carmen is that she was a swimmer,' said Perry.

'We haven't proved that,' said Susan. 'We're assuming she told the truth. We haven't proved it. She's not been a competitor in the UK.'

'Maybe we should find out where she has been competitive,' said Macleod. 'See if she was capable of jumping off that cliff edge?'

'The attacker was a serious swimmer. They could swim,' said Perry. 'I would just be bounced about in that water. And though it was tough, they were making their way. They had been in proper seas.'

'Agree with that,' said Macleod. 'What else did you find out?' he said to Susan.

'The Achterbergs meeting seemed to have been pretty bland. My contact said that Ludlow was charming, but Mrs Achterberg wasn't interested. And she chatted. Same with Mr Achterberg. Most things seem to be a quite light-hearted discussion. However, when I talked to one waitress, she said there was a moment when Ludlow didn't quite proposition her but was heading that way. She said Mr Achterberg jumped in, and actually reprimanded Ludlow for what he was doing.'

'In what way?' asked Perry.

'Forcibly. Very, very directly.'

'How did Ludlow react?' asked Macleod.

'He pulled back, the waitress said. However, she said that Ludlow tried when he was leaving to ask her out.'

'You've got to give the boy points for trying, haven't you?' said Perry. 'It's like he's been after nearly every woman he's come across.'

'He does, doesn't he?' said Macleod. 'And he was successful with one. But he was after the waitress as well.'

'I wonder,' said Ross. 'What does Tabitha think of his playing around? Does she know? You can't be that overt all the time and her not know.'

'You'd be surprised,' said Susan.

'True,' said Perry. 'We used to have Jenkins. Do you remember him, Seoras? Down in Glasgow.'

'He wasn't the worst of coppers,' said Macleod. 'But he was the worst of men. Especially where women were concerned.'

'You threw him out of a house once,' said Perry. 'Said he was making eyes at a victim's spouse.'

'He was. Whatever everybody gets up to outside of work, that's their business. As long as it's legal,' said Macleod. 'Inside of work, you don't flirt with potential victims and those left behind with a tragedy. They're vulnerable. Too easily, they'll grab onto somebody. A lifeline in the storm.'

'It's funny you should mention that,' said Susan. 'Gail Harmon's meeting. Apparently, she was dressed in a way never seen before.'

'So the people in the restaurant knew her?' asked Ross.

'She used to go out once a week and dine alone. Very straightforward. Jeans, jumper, something like that. Never smart. Always quick.

'That night she went out and Ludlow was with her,' said Susan. 'However, she was wearing a dress. And I talked to one waitress. She said she'd never ever seen Gail Harmon showing any cleavage until that night. She said the dress was short. And she said she looked great for it. It wasn't a case of looking like meat on the shelf. She said she looked very attractive, very tasteful, and yet very alluring.'

'Made a big effort,' said Macleod.

'She did, and Ludlow was all over her,' said Susan. 'It was rather an intimate meeting, and then they were seen getting into the same taxi.'

'Well, she openly admits they went back to her flat,' said Perry. 'So, we kind of knew they were all over each other.'

'And then he disappears,' said Macleod. He looked up at the ceiling for a moment, and then over at Perry. 'What did you say about Mr Dawes, Perry?'

'Mr Dawes is the neighbour of Gail Harmon. 'He's been watching her, keeping an eye.'

'Did he see her that night?' asked Macleod. Apparently, he's been watching what's going on with her, so a potential source, do you think? We might need a bit more on Gail Harmon's life.'

'I can look,' said Perry.

'Let me do that,' said Macleod.

'So where are we at?' said Ross, after all that.

'Well, we're looking for a female,' said Macleod. 'A female who can truly swim. Who have we got?'

'Well,' said Susan. 'Selina can't. At least not well. Carmen can. Jealousy kills Ludlow. It's possible.'

'You've also got Gail Harmon. She reacted really badly,'

said Perry, 'when we told her about Ludlow being attached. Perhaps she found that out before she heard it from us. Did she react? Maybe it was her first time in a long time, and then suddenly that's just blown away. Did she think there was something more than a one-night stand?'

'She is a swimmer,' said Macleod. 'A proper swimmer.'

'That's true. The Achterbergs—Mrs Achterberg will swim nowhere,' said Ross. 'From what you said?'

'No,' said Macleod. 'I don't see it. They had a daughter, but I don't know where she is.'

'There's one other person,' said Perry.

'Who?' asked Macleod.

'Tabitha. She could swim. That's why she was with Ludlow. Met through competitions.'

'True, but she's awfully far out of it. We have seen nothing for her to be involved. Why up here?' asked Macleod.

'Maybe here is when she found out,' said Perry. 'He's obviously a bit of a scumbag. Jumping around between women.'

'All conjecture,' said Ross. 'We need some hard evidence.'

'Sergeant, you're right,' said Macleod. 'We know it's a female. Let's make sure we concentrate on them. I think I'm going to talk to Carmen and Selina. I need to find out what's up with her. Perry, you're with me. Susan, get the search wrapped up. Ross, you need to come back with something, or I'm going to switch off that computer.'

Ross glanced up at Macleod. 'Yes, sir!'

Chapter 16

Macleod had felt damp in his coat after being out in the hail when he recovered his fedora. He now looked a little strange with a waterproof jacket on over his jumper and shirt and the fedora back on his head. He probably should have put the beanie on. That would have made more sense. But the hat had become a part of him now. He thought it gave him a sense of style.

That was how Jane had changed him. Macleod had never thought about style. Never. But she gave him style. She told him what looked good. She had told him she liked that hat. If there was ever proof that she was someone who could control Macleod, that was it. The man who didn't bother with style, the man who was dressed neatly for the job, suddenly had a touch of panache.

He looked across at Perry in the driver's seat beside him. Perry had his own style. It was slovenly, yes. He always had a jacket on that didn't seem to really fit him, a shirt that did nothing to flatter his figure. Perry also surprised you out of that slovenly look.

Macleod thought back to the rocks. He'd had the killer standing over him, putting him on the floor, and then turning back to Jimbo. Jimbo would have been a goner, except Perry flung himself—an almighty sack of potatoes that pummelled into her back. And he got up as if it was nothing. Even now, he didn't look for any respect from doing it. He was just Perry.

'She's doing well, isn't she?' said Macleod.

'Who?' asked Perry.

'Susan. She's doing well, taking to the leg.'

'She says it hurts. She's not as quick as she was. Not as stable. She doesn't walk the same,' said Perry.

'Well, how can you?'

'But it bothers her,' said Perry. 'Behind it all, it bothers her. I think she's happier when it's not on. When she's able to kick about the house. I think she feels almost freer then.'

'What do you mean?'

'She wears the trousers down,' continued Perry. 'Before, when she was out and about in town, Susan might have had a skirt. She liked to show her legs off. And now she hides it. The metal pin coming down out of her knee. She feels a need to hide it. She's almost freer without it, except she'd have to use those crutches.'

'You think she's going to be okay?' asked Macleod.

'She's strong. And she's happy because she can move about. She can do her work again,' said Perry. 'It's just that, well, she's still grieving behind it all.'

Macleod sat back. *All I have seen is a woman who is coping, a woman who is getting on. Perry was so astute with people. He won't have asked her either*, he thought. *He'll have just noticed the little things.*

Perry pulled the car back up in front of the house of Selina and Carmen, and together with Macleod, approached the door.

It was opened, and once again, the feeling of a sauna getting let loose came flooding through that door. Macleod could feel himself wanting to step inside quickly, so cold was it outside. Before them stood Carmen. She was dressed this time in a t-shirt and shorts.

'Detective Inspector and—'

'Constable Perry,' Perry said resignedly.

'I was wondering if I could have a talk to Selina and you,' said Macleod.

'Of course. Just a moment; she's working on something. Come in.' Carmen led them through to the sitting room they'd been in before.

Macleod sat down, taking in the room while they waited for Selina to enter. When she did, she was wearing a long but light, colourful, blue skirt, and an orange blouse with her springy black hair in evident attendance. It was like a wild mop, but Macleod thought, attractive and natural. It gave the essence of being free, not styled for looks. Not held back by anything.

She took a seat while Carmen sat down beside Perry on the long sofa. Macleod had been given a chair of his own.

'I just wanted to come and ask you about your meal with Ludlow,' Macleod said to Selina. 'Once again, how did it go?'

'It went well. We discussed some things. A little more light-hearted by then,' said Selina. 'We'd given the day to discussing all about the business, so it was good to relax a little.'

'And you were there on your own for a while with him,' said Macleod.

'Yes,' said Selina.

Macleod noted Carmen was watching closely, almost hanging on every word that was said.

'Mr Ludlow has been said to be a bit of a flirt,' said Macleod. 'On the previous day, he had dined with another woman and taken her to bed. Prior to that, he's seen as being flirtatious. He also tried to chat up your waitress, I believe. Did he make any advances on you?'

Selina sat back for a moment. 'Well, he was charming. He was certainly—'

'He was being more than charming,' said Carmen. 'Man was practically drooling over you.'

'I wouldn't say that,' said Selina.

'I would. Drooling. I was ready to get up and hit him. But you encouraged him anyway.'

'What do you mean "I encouraged him?"' said Selina.

'With what you were wearing.'

'Excuse me,' said Selina. 'I wasn't the one who came in parading the flesh.'

'Well, you didn't look, did you?' said Carmen. 'You were all for him; all eyes were on him.'

Selina stood up. 'I will not sit here and listen to that.'

Carmen stood up to match her, standing in front of her. 'You will listen. You'll listen to me. I've given up everything to be here with you. I've come all this way. And you do what you do—'

'What do you think we are?' said Selina.

'You know what we are. You know what we've been—'

'Can I ask,' said Macleod, 'where were you earlier today? This morning?'

Carmen glared at him. 'Why?'

'I asked a question,' said Macleod.

'She's been with me,' said Selina.

'Really?' said Macleod.

'Yes.' Selina put her hand on Carmen's shoulder, but Carmen slipped behind her, wrapping her arms around her. Macleod wasn't the most intimate of men, but he recognised someone who was struggling with an intimate showing. Selina wasn't happy with what had been done. She'd put an arm up, a show of solidarity, backing Carmen. But Carmen had slid round, like they were lovers.

Macleod wondered, *Had they been? Were they? Ludlow would have been a threat.*

'Did you not like Mr Ludlow making approaches to Selina?' asked Macleod.

'I don't like any men that make that sort of approach to a woman, especially a sleazy slime bucket like him. But we needed the business; otherwise, I wouldn't have touched him with a barge pole.'

'He wasn't that bad,' said Selina. 'Besides, I can handle myself.'

'You were handling yourself with him. That was the problem,' said Carmen.

Selina opened Carmen's arms, stepping away. 'You don't get to speak to me like that. You don't get to—'

'Once again,' said Macleod, 'where were you, Miss Cabral, this morning?'

'Right here, in this house.'

'And you can confirm that, Miss Soto?'

'Yes,' she said. 'Absolutely.'

Perry suddenly excused himself and made for the door. Macleod turned back to the two women.

'I have two people dead now, both men. I will find whoever has harmed them. Do you own blue leggings, a blue fleece, or a balaclava?' Macleod asked Carmen.

'Got a blue fleece,' she said.

'Can you show me it?'

She took him through to a rear bedroom. From a wardrobe,

144

she pulled out a blue fleece. It wasn't quite the right colour.

'Do you own a balaclava at all?'

'What am I?' said Carmen. 'A terrorist? I don't come from the Basque region.'

'Have you been swimming today?'

'We swim every day. Both of us.'

'Even today?' Macleod asked.

'I went for a short swim. Sea was rough. Not that rough, though. Not in the bay.'

Macleod nodded, and as Carmen led him back out of the bedroom, he took a glance back. The bed wasn't made, and it was a double. However, from what he could tell, there was only one indentation, one groove. As he walked back up the corridor, he glanced into an open door on the left; a smaller bedroom with a single bed that was also not fully made. He wondered, were they not as close as Carmen wanted? Had there been a row? Had there been trouble?

He almost wished Perry was looking at this, to get his insight, but he hadn't come back into the house after disappearing outside.

'Can you confirm that Carmen and you were off swimming this morning?' he said to Selina.

'We swim every morning,' she said. 'Always. It's good experience for me. It gets me used to what clients will do in case Carmen ever got unwell. I try to show her the business side, too.'

'What is your exact relationship?' Macleod asked Selina.

'We're friends,' said Selina. 'Friends and business partners.'

Macleod looked at Carmen. There was a fire in her eyes.

'Very good friends,' she almost spat out. 'Close,' she said.

'Like sisters,' Selina said back.

The tension between the two women was strong, and Macleod felt almost awkward being this far into a relationship and seeing the strains of it. It was his job, of course, to understand anything that could affect the case but sometimes he felt like an intruder.

Perry returned to the room and whispered in Macleod's ear.

'Girl missing from the local area. Paula Huntly. Her older sister's just reported it.'

'You think this is—'

'I don't know,' said Perry. 'It could be. It's worth a look.'

'Could be something unrelated,' Macleod whispered back. 'That being said, it needs investigating. Tell Susan to liaise with the search team and get people moving to look for the girl. We'll finish up here and then try to work out if this Paula Huntley is anything of interest to us. We'll also pop round and see her sister. How long has she been missing?'

'Couple of days, we think,' said Perry. 'Fits in. It fits in with Danny Poland going missing. Blonde hair, too.'

Macleod got an uneasy feeling in his stomach. He turned back to the women and saw that Selina and Carmen had now sat down in seats far away from each other. He wondered if there'd been whispered words while he was receiving the report from Perry.

'I have to go, but I may be back. Don't go anywhere.'

He walked out of the house, but before he got into the car, he made a point of checking the car driven by Carmen and Selina. There only appeared to be one, and it was red. He made a note of the number plate before getting in beside Perry.

'I've got a bad feeling,' said Macleod.

'About the girl?'

'Very much. I also got a feeling about these two. It's not

146

them. I don't see it,' said Macleod. 'Two together. Maybe not like they should be. But they do things together. They're swimming together this morning. Even after all that rowing. Even after Ludlow makes an approach.'

'They still go swimming in the morning, but end up with all that nonsense instead of just having a huff. They don't sleep together though, do they?' said Perry.

'What makes you say that?'

'Look at the way they are. I think Carmen wants them to. Remember, they were closer in the past. That was mentioned in the conversation if not explicitly,' said Perry. 'Maybe that's what it's come from, and then somebody didn't want that type of relationship. I mean, they've got a business reason to be together. They had little to say to that, did they?'

'They sleep in different beds from what I saw when she took me to look at her fleece. Or at least certainly did last night,' said Macleod.

'Well, you might be right,' said Perry. 'In the meantime, let's go find our missing girl.'

He pulled the car out of the drive, heading back along the coast road. Macleod sat looking out at the grey storm clouds whizzing past. The hail had stopped for the moment, but it would be back, for it was that kind of day.

The car, during the short time they'd been inside, had cooled down, and Macleod turned up the heating and put on the fan. He was definitely getting old. He was a Scotsman, after all. The cold never bothered him before.

Chapter 17

Macleod returned to the police station where he found Susan Cunningham in an unfamiliar room with members of the search community. He stood at the door for a moment until he caught her eye, and then she followed him out a couple of minutes later. In the corridor, he asked her, 'So what's it looking like?'

'They're pulling in the last sightings of her. By the looks of it, the neighbours saw her disappear. I've indicated to them about the jewellers and that we are checking it. We're struggling after that. We're going through bus and other CCTV, see if she can be spotted anywhere, but we are struggling. Not many sightings of her, so they're covering off all the usual places.'

'Check in sea caves as well?'

'Best we can. It's not always easy. There's actually quite a lot of coast to cover,' said Susan.

'Well, keep on it,' said Macleod. 'Don't let them let up.'

'They don't,' said Susan abruptly.

'I know,' said Macleod. 'But you have to keep at it. Keep feeding them information. Especially anything else we dig up. I fear for that girl.'

'You think she's still alive?' asked Susan.

'She's either hiding out somewhere, struggling to find somewhere secure, or somebody she can trust, or she's been got to already,' said Macleod. 'In either case, it's not good.'

'Do we know who our killer is yet? Do we have any real ideas?'

'Honestly, no. We know it's a woman. That's all we know,' admitted Macleod.

'You know it was a female attacker that chased the other lad. That's what we know,' said Susan.

Macleod stopped abruptly. He was about to say something, because in truth it was cheeky. Then he didn't. 'You're absolutely right,' he said. 'You're absolutely right.'

'A strong swimmer, though,' said Susan.

'I need Ross to come through with some more information. We're very light on people's backgrounds.'

'It's where he's strongest,' said Susan. She went to say something, but then she didn't.

'What?' asked Macleod.

'It's not my place to say.'

'I'm not Hope. I'm the big boss. You're about to say something. You can't withdraw like that. Say it. I'll tell you if it's not your place to say.'

'Well, the thing is, Hope lets Ross stay there, you know? I'd have thought that probably would have been my role, or Perry's, to do the digging like that. Perry's not good on that front. He's not great with computers. But we can still head up a team. I thought with my injury that's where I was going to get stuck.'

'You can move about all right, can't you?' asked a concerned Macleod.

'I'd be lying if I said I was as good as I was before. But I can move. I'm learning to run on it. That takes a bit of getting used to. Can't go fast.'

'What about in a scrap? You think you can still take people on?'

'I'm going to get some training. Hope said she could put me in touch with someone.'

'Did she indeed?' said Macleod, and he had an idea who Hope intended. 'By the way,' he said, 'it's not your place to call that. But I'm glad you did.'

'Is Hope coming to join us in the next couple of days?' asked Susan. 'I know she was only meant to be on leave until tomorrow.'

'That depends on what happened when she was away. She wasn't just taking time out. I can't say anymore.'

'Something wrong with her baby?' asked Susan.

Macleod raised his eyebrows and gave his head a shake. 'I can't say anything about that. That's why she's not here. Otherwise, I'd have pulled her away from her leave for this one.'

He turned away, and went to find Ross. He was sitting behind his computer.

'Sergeant, come on. We need to talk to this girl's sister. Find out what's been going on.'

'I'm just—'

'Stuck on the computer again. I said you're with me,' said Macleod.

'Yes, sir.'

'Perry,' said Macleod over his shoulder to Perry in the corner, 'get down to the jewellers. Get a photograph of Paula Huntley. See if it's the same girl. Make sure that's confirmed. If it is, she's not just a missing girl. She's being hunted, I would suspect.'

Perry nodded and shambled in his usual fashion out the door. Ross was soon ready and came with Macleod down to the car. As they sat, with Ross driving, Macleod could feel an air of tension.

'What's the matter, Ross?' he asked.

'Nothing.'

'I've been a detective for how long? I can tell something's wrong. It's pretty obvious. What's the matter?'

'I've got work on the computer to do.'

'And? I've asked you to be with me. You're the sergeant here. I need you with me in this interview. This interview. This is important, this bit.'

'With all due respect, sir, it's all important.'

'And I deem this to be the most important bit at this time.'

'Yes, sir.'

Macleod turned to look out the window. *Ross hadn't been himself ever since he'd started a family. He seemed to see things differently, wanted things a certain way. That didn't always work out,* Macleod thought. He'd never had family himself, but then again, his life had been smashed to pieces before it had begun with his wife. He was just thankful he'd got another chance now with Jane.

He turned to Ross. 'You're a sergeant now. You can't just sit on a computer. You need to have Perry or Susan taking that role.'

'With all due respect, sir, they haven't got my skills.'

'With all due respect, Ross, you deal with that. There's plenty of people in the station who can handle computers as well as you. You co-opt them. And you get Perry or Susan to be in charge of them. They know what they're looking for. The other people can tell them how to look for it.'

'Sir.'

Macleod sighed for a moment. Then he said, 'Ross, you became a sergeant to develop and grow. All I see is you stepping back into being the computer junkie. As soon as I come on board, you want to make coffee for me again. That's not you anymore. You've got to grow and develop, Alan. You've got to step up to the next level. Like Hope has.'

'She's happy with me there. She's—'

'And if you keep it like that, Perry will get to be a sergeant. When Perry gets to be a sergeant, you'll no longer be the sergeant in the team. That's a waste. You'll be overqualified for what you're doing. You need to be getting into the cases at a higher level. I'm telling you this for your own good.'

'With all due respect, DI McGrath does not see it that way.'

'With all due respect, DI McGrath's view of it is my business. At the moment, I'm on this case, so you're doing what you should do with me. You were brilliant at what you did. That's why I want you to go up higher. You'll be brilliant again. Get that into your thick skull,' said Macleod.

It was unusual of Macleod. Almost tetchy. He was worried for the girl, absolutely. He was bothered about the way Ross was, yes. But these days he was less assured, or less quiet. Maybe that was it.

Jane said he was becoming the grumpy git everybody thought he was, attuning into the role at times. Macleod thought he'd mellowed. And around Jane he certainly was. He'd even raced off to Italy to look after Susan. That'd have been an eye-opener. But he saw Ross not achieving his full potential. He saw Ross struggle with the family, not knowing what he should be.

He couldn't be the mother who catered to the entire team.

He had to be a sergeant, a wingman for Hope. Macleod folded his arms, but Ross said nothing as they continued to drive to Paula Huntley's house.

When they arrived, Macleod could see several constables already there. They led him into the living room of the house and introduced Fiona Huntley. She looked scared. Extremely scared.

'Miss Huntley, I'm Detective Chief Inspector Macleod. This is Detective Sergeant Alan Ross. Your sister's in grave trouble, I think. I need to know everything about what happened.'

'She's gone!'

'What happened? Where were you?'

'I was at my boyfriend's, okay? His parents had gone away, so I told Paula just to stay here.'

Blimey, thought Macleod. *So, she popped away to get a little bit of intimacy and privacy with her boyfriend. And now her sister's missing.*

'Did Paula have any boyfriends?'

'No,' said Fiona. 'Paula's a dweeb. Paula wouldn't bother with boys. Paula . . . well, she just . . . she didn't go in for that sort of thing.'

'Is she quiet?' asked Macleod.

'Very,' said Fiona.

'When are your parents back?' asked Macleod.

'They were meant to come . . . they give us a lot of free rein. I'm eighteen, you know,' said Fiona.

'Paula was sixteen,' said Macleod.

'Yes, she can look after herself, like me. Only she hasn't this time, has she?' The girl turned and almost hugged the cushion on the sofa.

'Is there anything else you can tell me about your sister? Any likely places she would go?'

'I didn't get on with the bitch! All right!'

Macleod rocked a little from that comment. But then he stepped outside the room with Ross and a constable.

'Inspector,' said the constable. 'She doesn't seem to know anything about her sister. Either that or she's just keeping everything locked in. It's very uncharacteristic, apparently.'

'Do we know anything else?' asked Macleod.

'Well,' said the constable, 'we've gone door to door around the neighbours. Paula was seen disappearing off with a small rucksack a few evenings ago.'

'And I take it hasn't been seen since?'

'No. Hasn't been seen at all. There's a woman about two doors down who seems to be a bit of a nosy-neighbour type. She said she'd seen a young man hanging about.'

'Did you show the photograph of Danny Poland?'

'Yes. She reckons it was him. Been seen a couple of times round here over the last couple of weeks. I think the two of them may have been running off together for a bit.'

'But why,' said Macleod, 'why go all the way out there? Why not just come here?'

'Nosy-neighbour syndrome, I think,' said the constable. 'From what I can gather, the neighbour's quite happy to tell Paula's mother and father about what goes on. She says they're useless, not fit for purpose. She has several times gone up and berated them about leaving Paula like this or whatever Fiona's done. That's probably why the two of them went off elsewhere. Because absolutely, you'd come here if you were alone. It's warm. You wouldn't go out to a cave.'

Macleod thanked the constable, and he stepped back outside the house. The hail wasn't falling at the moment, but it was cold. A dampness to the air, too. Ross stood beside Macleod.

'Shall I get back to the office? Get stuck into—'

'Who's that?' said Macleod and saw a car approaching.

'That's like the inspector's car,' said Ross.

'Our inspector,' said Macleod. 'I think it is.'

The car pulled up on the roadside outside the house. The door opened and a woman in a long coat stepped out. Her hair was tied up in a ponytail at the back and was a stark colour of red. She looked over at Macleod with a faint smile.

'You can get back in the car,' said Macleod to Ross. 'Back to the station and do whatever you want to dig up stuff. I'm going to bring somebody else up to speed.'

Macleod stood and watched as Hope passed Ross, giving him a quick hello and a nod before making her way towards Macleod. There was a long winter's coat on, but underneath were the boots that Macleod was so familiar with seeing her wear. There were jeans there too, and she smiled as she approached.

'How are things?' asked Macleod.

'Things are okay, a bit of a scare, but it's okay. We're good to go, both of us. We're fine.'

'And John?'

'John's worried sick, but he's okay. How are you doing here?'

'We're still behind the drag curve on it,' said Macleod. 'I've got a missing girl who may already be dead. Either that or scared witless and hiding out. It's cold, it's pouring at times, not a place for her to be. Susan's doing well on her new leg. She's coordinating; she's helping me with the search. Perry's off checking to see if we can confirm the movements of the girl we're hunting for. And on the way over in the car, I just chewed Ross out about not getting his backside into gear. Something

155

I need to have a go at you for also.'

Hope looked astonished. 'I was on holiday. Holiday? I was—'

'Not about that. No problem with that,' said Macleod. 'I'm glad you're well. Let's head for the car, and I'll explain to you. You give me a rundown of your situation, then I'll update you about the case when we get to the station. On the way there, I'll update you about Ross. You see, Hope, when you're the boss, you have to bring people on. You're not doing it with Ross.'

'He's been mardy, difficult. He's happy in his place researching.'

'He is happy in his place. And he's useful in his place,' said Macleod. 'You were happy. You were useful in your place as my sergeant. But you were born to be an inspector. You've got all the ability. If truth be told, I'd be happier being the inspector. We were a good team. But that would have been an injustice to you. And an injustice to the force. Can't make that mistake with Alan. He's too good.'

'Part of me thinks I should have stayed off,' said Hope.

She went round to the side of her car, clambered in, and Macleod clambered in the passenger seat. She went to turn the key, but he reached over with his hand, stopping her. He turned in the seat, reached forward, pulled her close to him, gave her a hug, and said in her ear, 'I'm glad it's all okay. Really glad.'

He broke off the hug, and she smiled. 'Not as much as me.'

Chapter 18

P erry stepped out of the jewellers with their worst fears confirmed. The jeweller identified Paula Huntley as the girl who had been with Danny Poland. It raised the stakes somewhat. She wasn't just missing; she was running or she was potentially dead.

Perry texted the confirmation message to Macleod and then returned to the station. As he walked along the corridor, he saw the search team's room and Susan liaising with the coordinator.

'What's happening?' he said.

'We're having a large search of the town and area. There's a lot of the general public come to be involved.'

'Where are you gathering?' asked Perry.

'It's down round the corner. It's a large public car park, so everybody can park their cars and walk out, start looking through the town.'

'Wooded areas and that sort of thing?' said Perry.

'Yes. Knock on doors, houses, have a look, see what else they can find. We're searching the sea caves as well but that's slow going. It's not easy to get into some of them. Some of them become inaccessible with the high tide. According to the Coastguard, the caves, some of them you can actually stay inside while the tide is high. But it seals off the entrance, unless you can swim in. It's not an easy place to search. So for some of them, they're waiting. You can't risk people—'

'Fair enough,' said Perry. Susan smiled at him. She went to turn to go with the team, but Perry put his hand out on her shoulder. 'You okay?' he said.

'Perry,' she said, 'we're in the middle of—'

'I know,' said Perry. 'I'm asking if you're okay. Your leg, it's all holding up? You're doing—'

'Perry, you're awful sweet. You really are. But I'm fine. Okay? Just be my friend. It's what I need at the moment.'

'Of course,' he said. He watched as she turned away, disappearing inside a different office. Part of him wondered what was for him. Would he ever see someone he could feel close to?

Susan had hit him out of nowhere. He never would have thought he'd have a chance with someone like that, and apparently that was the case. But even when she was injured, he just wanted to be around her. In truth, he'd given up the cigarettes because he knew she didn't like them. And even after she said that she wasn't interested in that type of relationship, and just to be colleagues, he hadn't gone back on them. Because he knew she still didn't like them.

I must be tired, he thought. *Things like this running through my head. Suddenly getting an emotional moment and reaching out to her.*

Susan came back out from the room, carrying a large coat. It was fluorescent and she walked up to him and handed it over.

'Says "Police" on the back. You should have one. Here, it's too cold to go around without one on. The boss said you were soaked, frozen when you chased after that lad.'

'Didn't have time, did I? I don't enjoy driving in big coats. I don't like—'

'But where is the issued coat? Your one?'

'I think it's in the locker at the station,' he said. 'It's not me—'

'Perry, it's perishing out there. Wear it. Wear it for me,' she said. Her hand went up and touched the side of his cheek, gently. 'You're a good friend, Perry. A really good friend.'

She took her hand down, walked off down the corridor, and Perry thought she was just being kind. But when she looked back over her shoulder, not once, but twice, it made him wonder. He was just being daft, hoping for something that wasn't there. She'd been through a lot.

He put the coat on and zipped it up. Inside was a pair of gloves as well, and he found a beanie hat in one of the other pockets. So equipped, he decided to walk out and see the start of the search. Maybe part of him just wanted to keep his eyes on Susan but there was something else behind it. He needed a break anyway. Some fresh air. It was part of his habit to step outside. Even though there were no cigarettes to step out for.

A few minutes later, Perry was standing in the car park looking at the assembled throng of people. There was a large number out and the search professionals were splitting them up. As Perry watched, he saw Mr Achterberg, along with Mrs Achterberg. They were geared up in proper wet-weather gear.

And across from them, he saw Gail Harmon. Beyond her was Tabitha Green. She was dressed up less like someone about to do a search than someone about to do their Christmas shopping. Her coat was stylish. She had knee-length boots. And in truth, she looked well. Gail Harmon, however, didn't look well. She was almost shivering, although she had winter-weather gear on.

Perry watched closely as Gail was moved across to one team. Mrs Achterberg was put in the team with her. And it looked like the constable was ushering Mr Achterberg there as well, but he split off into another group. Perry noted that Tabitha Green was in that group as well. Perry looked at Mrs Achterberg, who almost blanked Gail.

They were a team of about eight people, but they never acknowledged each other. They simply didn't seem to know each other. Perry found that strange. If you were setting up one of these swimming groups, you'd probably know who was alongside you. It wasn't a massive run between them. Surely you'd have gone along and jumped in with that group. You'd have checked out the competition. Perry was a little bit bemused at the complete lack of knowledge of each other.

He saw everyone was about to make a move and that Gail looked almost penitent in her efforts for the group. Perry stepped forward, spoke to one of the search consultants and said he'd be taking Gail for a moment, asking where she could catch up.

So advised, he stepped up and said, 'Gail Harmon, hello again. Detective Constable Perry. Can I have a word?' She stepped to one side with him. 'Out searching, then?' he said.

'Least I can do, isn't it?' said Gail. 'I mean, this girl, she's tied into all of this. Well, I just feel somehow I'm, well, I don't know, partly responsible. I went to bed with the man.'

'That you did. Was it all sweetness and light, though?'

'How do you mean?' she said.

'You went out to dinner. You spent all day with the man. When did you decide it would be a good idea to go to bed?'

'Beg your pardon,' said Gail.

'Forgive me,' said Perry, 'but looking at it from his point of view, given the way he obviously wanted to get into bed with you, there was nobody else around. Afternoon after concluding business, why even bother with dinner? Why not push you there and then? That's what I don't get. Seen it before.'

'Have you been talking to Dawes?' she said.

'We briefly spoke to Dawes. Why?'

'Shouldn't say—'

'You absolutely should say,' said Perry. He didn't know what she should say or what she was talking about. One of the thoughts running through his mind at that point in time was how good the gloves he was wearing were in stopping him from feeling the cold, but he forced himself to focus.

'We went to dinner because that's what was planned,' said Gail. 'When we were conducting the business, we swam in the morning, but I didn't simply bring him back. We came back briefly, looked at the numbers, and then took him out for a walk. On the way, we stopped at a coffee shop. When we came back after that, he asked to come up.'

'He asked to come up. What did you say?' asked Perry.

'I asked if he was with someone. He said that didn't matter. He said she didn't matter. She was nothing special. That I was much more.'

'You went for that?' said Perry. 'You don't strike me like a woman who would go for that.'

'It's been so long. So long since intimacy. So long since, well, since my husband died. I wanted him. Do you understand that, Mr Perry? I wanted him.'

Perry understood, all right. He had his own longings. But that wasn't helping him at the moment.

'You wanted him. So what happened? You've come back towards the flat. Why didn't you just take him up and there you go? Bob's your uncle.'

'We were going to go up, and I said no. Let's make it tonight. I wanted it to be classier,' said Gail. 'He was all in the moment but I wanted to savour it. I wanted him. God knows I wanted him, but I wanted him to see me as a woman, not this business venture person. I was dressed in my jeans and a jumper. That night at dinner, I was dressed properly. He was forceful, though. He was insistent on going up.'

'So, how did you get him away that afternoon?' asked Perry.

'There was a shout from a nearby car. I don't know who that was. It seemed to disturb him, though.'

'Right,' said Perry. 'You think it was his girlfriend? Or do you think it was someone else?'

'I don't know who it was. But they had company.'

'How do you mean?' asked Perry.

'Because there were two voices. There was a man and there was a woman.'

'From the same car? From the same place?'

'I don't know,' said Gail. 'It came from the same general direction, but whether they were together or what, I don't know, but they must have been. I couldn't have two people watching me, could I? Two people watching us. Watching him. I mean, how does that work? Maybe she brought her own private detective with her.'

'But he left?' said Perry.

'Yes, he left at that point. Sharpish. Came back that night in a taxi. Met me in the restaurant. We got a taxi home to my place.'

Gail reached up and put a hand atop her chest. Perry could

see she was breathing harder now, the memory bringing back excitement.

'It might have been just a moment for him, but it was release for me. It was a freedom. It was stepping out. Do you get that?'

'I might do,' said Perry. 'Very possibly. You should have told us this at the start.'

'I didn't want to ruin it. It was my moment with him. I didn't want to see him as the forceful type. He was,' said Gail. 'I look back and I think he just wanted me for my body. Just wanted to conquer me. One of these male arses. I didn't want that. I wanted someone that wanted this. Well, what was I? A vixen? I like that idea,' she said. 'I like that idea. And with a man from far away, I could play it.'

'You better get back to your search,' said Perry. 'I'll inform the chief inspector about your earlier omissions.'

He watched her go, and in truth, part of Perry felt for her. He was lonely. Not everybody who was single was as lonely. But he was, and clearly Gail Harmon was. Other people seemed to manage on their own. Perry wasn't sure how.

He turned to walk back to the station and saw Susan talking with one of the search advisors out in the cold. She saw him staring and gave him a smile. As she turned back to do her job, Perry left, not wanting to look like he was staring. It took him maybe ten steps to get past the glow that was forming inside him, to get past the smile he'd just seen. But when he did, there was an alarm bell ringing in Perry's head.

A man and a woman both shouting. A man and a woman telling Ludlow and Gail Harmon to break up, to not be doing what they were about to do. Two people watching.

Who were those people? Two people made little sense, thought Perry. You wouldn't come with your detective. If you were a girlfriend wanting to see if your partner was cheating, you'd either do that yourself or you'd get the detective to do it and he'd report back to you.

Something was wrong here. He was seeing it from the wrong angle. He'd go and sit down for a bit for he needed to see this the right way. Something inside him told him this was the key to understanding what was happening.

Chapter 19

Macleod looked over at his tall, red-headed inspector and gave a smile. It was good to have Hope about again. She gave a different side to the investigation than he did. The others were great, but Hope and Macleod had formed such a partnership, it was hard to break away from it.

'Nearly got the coffee ready,' he said.

'You mean Ross hasn't been champing at the bit to get you it?'

'I don't allow him. He's a sergeant and he shouldn't be doing this bit. He should be busy.'

'You shouldn't be doing it either. You're the lead man, the head honcho,' said Hope.

'It gives me time to think,' said Macleod. 'I never realised that. If you want to get away from someone, or a team, do something. But make it mundane. Make it look like it's not involved with the investigation. But here, when I make coffee, I can think.'

They were standing in the tiny kitchenette of the police station, and they both turned around to the door when they heard a voice.

'That's me,' said Perry, and then the sudden, 'Oh, hello.'

'Hi Perry,' said Hope.

'Just a flying visit, then?' asked Perry.

'Didn't think you had enough bosses,' said Hope.

'You good?' asked Perry. It was his polite way of being intrusive, Macleod thought. He was worried about Hope. They all were when she had to disappear on a short holiday. This baby was turning into a team baby in a way that Ross's adoption of a young child never did. Macleod wasn't sure that was entirely fair either way. But that's what was happening.

'I'm fine, Perry. What about yourself? I hear you've been throwing yourself around again.'

'You weren't here to look after him,' said Perry, smiling. 'I'll have one.'

'Yes, sir,' said Macleod to Perry. He simply gave a laugh.

'He seems okay,' said Hope quietly to Macleod.

'Perry, he's fine.'

'What about Susan?'

'Seems okay.,' said Macleod. 'May be getting used to this new prosthetic. She's coping well. She'll be last back, I reckon.'

'She's staying very close to the search teams.'

Perry took a couple of the coffees and turned to walk out of the kitchenette, when a blonde-haired woman popped her head in.

'Hope!' said Susan. She stepped forward and put her arms around Hope and gave her a quick hug. 'You look well. You are well, aren't you?'

'For the record,' said Hope, 'I'm fine.'

'I haven't got long, Seoras,' Susan said to Macleod. 'I need to get back out again.'

'Well, let's get going then,' said Macleod. 'There.' He reached a coffee round to Susan. 'In we go.'

The four of them entered the small room that was being commandeered by the murder team and sat around a table. Ross joined them and Macleod pulled them to order.

'With Perry's discovery, I think we need to take a second look at what's in front of us.'

'And that would be?' asked Susan.

'Well,' said Perry, 'I talked to Gail Harmon. Gail was a little economical with the truth. During the afternoon, after they conducted a bit of business, they went out to a coffee shop. After, they came back to her flat and they were going to— well, see they were going to—Ludlow was pushing her to head upstairs and get a bit more intimate. They were interrupted by a voice, two voices in fact—a female and a male—shouting at them. Ludlow disappeared, and they met up again for dinner that night. That's when, well, they went to bed.'

'They were being watched then,' said Hope.

'I've phoned Mr Dawes since then. He doesn't remember that bit. Not to say it didn't happen,' said Perry.

'She could fake it, though,' said Ross. 'This could be a way of trying to cover up her own tracks.'

'It could be,' said Perry. 'I didn't get that feeling. She doesn't seem the sort of person who could pull off this act. It's just an opinion. It's a little strange though she didn't talk about this the first time. And that's bothering me,' said Perry. 'It's conflicting with what I'm seeing and what I'm hearing from her.'

'Could the voices be the Achterbergs?' asked Ross.

'Why?' asked Macleod. 'I don't get that, Ross. Why on earth would the Achterbergs be there watching?'

'Is Gail Harmon anything to the Achterbergs?' asked Hope.

'I know I'm late into the investigation, so keep me up to speed.'

'Not that we're aware of,' said Macleod. 'In fact, the only thing we seem to know about them and her is that we've got two potentially rival franchises. Although, there's nothing to say that any of these franchises were being rejected in favour of the other.'

'Awfully close together, though, aren't they?' said Hope. 'I mean, how many people do you need to make a franchise run? How many people need to be in your group? Is it pin money?'

'Some of these franchise groups are quite big, fifty or sixty people going into the water at once,' said Ross. 'Although I'm not sure it's that big up here. Within his franchise, however, he has other groups that are quite small. He seems to have positioned it so you can grow as big as you want, stay as small as you want.'

'So there's actually no real reason here, is there?' asked Macleod.

'What about Tabitha?' said Susan. 'Maybe she had a man with her. Maybe she spotted him.'

'Maybe, but why not just come out? Why not hunt him down? And who's this other guy?' said Macleod. 'If it's a detective with her, you don't do that. You take the photographs, you get the evidence. You wouldn't shout out, would you?'

'But it could be Tabitha with someone,' said Susan. 'We haven't really ruled her out yet, have we?'

'We haven't really ruled anybody out,' said Macleod.

'We're going to be looking for Paula most of the night,' said Susan. 'We've got lots of teams out, lots of local people.'

'On that,' said Perry, 'Gail and the Achterbergs don't seem to know each other. Well, actually, to be more accurate, Mrs Achterberg and Gail don't seem to know each other. They're not that far apart, so they could have seen each other about, but when they were put together in a team for searching . . . they didn't even give a mutual nod. Nothing. Nothing to say they knew each other.'

'But Mr Achterberg seemed to know her,' said Macleod.

'He went off on a different team, Seoras,' said Perry. 'Which I found quite weird. I thought he would have been with his wife. But he was in with Tabitha's team. In fact, I thought he tried to manoeuvre himself there. The others seemed to just get placed.'

'Well,' said Ross, 'our two foreigners don't seem to want to join in the search.'

'They'll be keeping right out of it,' said Perry. 'Or watching it from a distance. Maybe we should check if they're in or not.'

'That's a thought, Ross. However, I think, Perry, you need to go back to Gail Harmon,' said Macleod. 'Pressure her as to why she didn't tell us.'

'Okay,' said Perry. 'I'll do that. I'll put the squeeze on her.'

'Go with him, Hope,' said Macleod.

'Okay,' said Hope, rather surprised. 'Because—'

'Because Constable Perry's brought Inspector McGrath with him. Put the squeeze on her, yes? Get a second opinion, then.'

'You're getting me to get a second opinion? This is Perry,' she looked over. 'The man you don't play poker with.'

Perry smiled. 'I get things wrong sometimes.'

'He does,' said Ross, to which Perry shot a glance.

'What have you come up with, Ross? Anything else?' Macleod said, quite severely.

'Still working on it. I've been talking to Europe, trying to find out a bit more about Carmen and Selina. Also making inquiries about the Achterbergs and Gail Harmon's past.'

'Well, carry on with it. We've got a lot of background not here,' said Macleod.

'I'm going to need to go in a minute,' said Susan. 'They're rendezvousing again before going back out.'

'Of course,' said Macleod. 'You can go.'

Susan stood up, grabbed her large jacket from where she'd hung it inside the office, and tore off out of the station. They could see Perry watching her go.

'You think our killer's after Paula as a witness, then?' said Hope.

'It all makes sense. I don't know how they're identifying who they think's seen them, though, said Perry.

'Danny Poland used to be part of the group of lads that found the cave,' said Macleod. 'We don't know if the killer was there, close to when the lads were there, and have extrapolated back to find what they think are witnesses. It was a very sharp and very quick effort when not a lot's been said.'

'What has been said?' asked Hope. 'What's the media know? What's out there? What would our killer know?'

Ross picked up his laptop, put it in front of Hope, and started bringing up various reports.

'Young persons mentioned,' said Hope. 'That's about it, isn't it? Young persons. Young men in the cave. Young persons.'

'But we brought them back out of the cave,' said Ross.

'They were rescued off by lifeboat,' said Macleod. 'The identity of the four of them wouldn't be difficult.'

'Might be a bit more difficult than that, though,' said Perry. 'Maybe they got a name. Maybe they didn't get all the names. You can't just batter into a lifeboat crew asking names, especially if you're not attached to that crew. You've got to drop in subtly. If the killer's not from around here, it makes it even more difficult. So maybe they got a name.'

'But that doesn't make sense either,' said Hope. 'If they got a name or a face, and they're from around here, maybe they'd seen a group. Was Danny Poland part of the group with the boys?'

'Yes,' said Macleod. 'They were actually worried about him. They called up about him.'

'And the others have said they've been seen. They've had people coming near them. Maybe somebody got hold of one name and then expanded it.'

'And then maybe they've seen Paula,' said Hope. 'With Danny, and that's why they're after Paula now too, in case Danny told her stuff, in case—'

'It's very clinical,' said Macleod, 'not like a rash murder. It's like somebody's trying to clean up afterwards, hinting towards professional, but not quite.'

'Very much,' said Perry.

'Well, there was the knife,' said Ross. 'Serrated—it was done in a professional manner.'

'But it's semi-professional,' said Macleod. 'Right idea, executed badly. A true pro, well, you would get the names, you'd be quiet, you wouldn't be seen tracking them, certainly not by boys.'

'So what are we saying then?' asked Hope. 'You think the murderer's local?'

'Possibly,' said Macleod. 'What I'm saying is it's definitely not a complete pro. It's not somebody brought in. So if somebody has . . . felt they've been spurned by Mr Ludlow, they haven't hired somebody to take him out. They've decided to take action themselves.'

'It'd be unlikely to be Tabitha then, wouldn't it?' said Ross.

'How's she going to know the locals? She's come in from afar. Even the names. It wouldn't work like that, would it? She wouldn't think Danny Poland is part of the group unless she'd seen them. But she wouldn't have seen them. It was after that, because Danny Poland wasn't with this group after the murder. He was part of the group before it.'

Macleod stood up, gave his head a shake. 'Going in circles this time,' he said. 'Right. Hope, Perry, go. Get a hold of Gail Harmon. She's out on the search. I'm not convinced about her.'

'I'll get back to my laptop then,' said Ross.

'I want answers, Ross,' said Macleod, 'and I want them fast.'

'Yes, sir.'

Ross turned away, back to his desk, carrying his laptop. Macleod saw Hope and Perry put on their jackets and leave. He'd stay in the room with Ross. Macleod walked out and off to the small kitchenette.

Something was bothering him. Semi-professional.

You didn't get semi-professional killers, thought Macleod. That just didn't make sense. So he wasn't looking at some sort of well-trained amateur. He was looking at somebody with some sort of training, but not particularly good training. And why did they yell out? What were they worried about? He thought back to what Perry had said.

Gail Harmon was standing with Ludlow. Ludlow was pressuring her to go inside. With somebody watching on, what would they see? What would they know? Did they get the feeling that this was it? He was going to take her upstairs and, well . . . the business would be done, so to speak. Did they shout out to interrupt? Did they shout out to stop it? But they didn't stop it later on that night. Why not? He was missing something.

And there was a man crying out, and a woman crying out. Why? Why would you both cry out? Why would you?

Unless, thought Macleod. *Unless . . .* He put two hands forward and leant on the kitchen top. Something was coming to mind. It wasn't clear. It wasn't completely clear.

And he wasn't completely sure of it. But he was getting an idea now. Of what may have happened there. It didn't fit the rest of the case yet, though. *I need pieces*, he thought. *I need pieces of the jigsaw. Ross, where's the pieces of the jigsaw? You're the only one not coming through with anything.'*

He wanted to go back in and sit in the office, but he decided not to. He thought about going outside to stand and think, but it was Baltic. As cold as it came. So instead, he stood in the kitchenette and poured himself some more coffee.

Chapter 20

Perry and Hope watched as the search teams reassembled, and a local van served out hot soup. After half an hour, the teams were ready to go again, but Perry intercepted Gail Harmon before they set off.

'Can I talk to you a moment?' asked Perry.

'Constable? Again?' said Gail. 'It's getting quite the late hour. I don't know if I'm going to be here much longer. I'm feeling the stress of it.'

'I can understand that,' said Perry. 'Can I take a moment, though?' He pointed to a lighted part of the car park, away from everyone.

She turned and followed him, arriving to see Hope coming out of the shadows. Because of the weather, Hope was dressed in a large, high-vis jacket, with the words 'POLICE' on the back of it. Her normally prominent red hair was covered by a black bobble hat. But she smiled as Gail approached.

'Let me introduce Detective Inspector Hope McGrath,' said Perry. 'Inspector, this is Gail Harmon, who we've spoken about.'

'Miss Harmon, I hope you don't mind us asking you a few questions.'

'Inspector,' said Gail. She almost reeled away from Hope. Like most people, she had to look up into Hope's eyes, being several inches shorter than her.

'I've been looking into reports from my colleagues, but something's bothering me,' said Hope.

'What's that?' asked Gail.

'Well,' said Perry. 'I told the inspector about the incident where Ludlow and you were going to go up to your—or rather, he was trying to force you up to your apartment—and you were shouted at.'

'Yes, I told you about that,' said Gail.

'You may have, but I don't understand,' said Hope. 'Why did you withhold that? It makes no sense. The man was dead.'

'I didn't want to become embroiled in his murder, so I told you about having sex with him. But, well, I wanted nothing more to come from it. I wanted to keep out of the way, you know. Those people who shouted, who knows who they were? Maybe they would come after me if I told you. And then I told you because, well, I needed to . . . I needed to get it off my chest. I had to tell you. It wasn't right to withhold it.'

'Well, that's correct,' said Hope. 'It wasn't right to withhold it. It looks highly suspicious. We've also talked to Mr Dawes. I believe you know him.'

Gail rolled her eyes, but she looked nervous.

'Mr Dawes says nothing about these shouts.'

'Well, they're real,' spat Gail agitatedly. 'I was there.'

'Don't raise your voice too high,' said Hope quietly. 'We don't want to bother the other searchers with this.'

'They are real,' said Gail resolutely. 'They shouted.'

'Tell me something,' said Hope. 'All of you here want to do wild swimming. Three franchises, as I understand, that

Ludlow visited. Why don't you all just get together and make one big one?'

'No, no. No, no,' said Gail. 'I can't do that. Anyone in mine has to be very special, has to be selected. I can't.'

'Because?' asked Hope.

'That's how he died. Did you get that?' said Gail. 'That's how he died. He went out to the sea. I need to know that the people going out, they know what they're doing. They know how to—'

'But surely larger numbers would mean more safety. According to reports I read, your husband died when he was out on his own.'

'I just need to have my group,' said Gail, her voice beginning to lift again.

'Okay,' said Hope. 'Easy. Don't say too much.'

'I don't go down to Strathy Bay, anyway. Okay? Don't go down that way. I have where I swim. Fresgoe is my bay. I don't go elsewhere. You know how hard it was to get back in the water? Do you know how hard it was to—' She stopped suddenly.

'Why are you out here?' asked Hope.

'Because this young girl is missing. We need to find her.'

'Do you know her?'

'I think I saw her about. I don't know her. Don't know the young people, but yes, you see them. Of course you would, about the area. Unlike some others, I have been here a long time. I got my life back together to a point where I could go out and swim,' said Gail. 'I got myself to a point where I swim with others. It's a small group, but I am back out in society. Yes? And then Ludlow comes along.

'It's like a dream. I loved the look of him. He was a swimmer too. He had that definition, that muscular tone that we have when you swim often. His body—'

Hope thought the woman was going to melt the way she was speaking about him. It was a dead man, after all. But she seemed to be caught up in an idea, a persona, a dream of him.

'He was something else. And when we talked, we talked about swimming. We talked about the business. I thought maybe—'

'You thought what?' asked Hope.

'Maybe if I opened up to him, if he saw me as a lover, a partner, he could have even settled up here. Run his franchises from out of here. He could come and be part of my world. I could—'

Hope watched as tears fell from the woman's eyes. She choked up, her hand going up to her face, gloves wiping at her eyes. She was shivering now, but not from the cold. Then she stopped and looked up at Hope, and whispered, 'Some bastard killed him. Some bastard killed him. If I get hold of them, do you know what I will do?'

'I think I get the idea,' said Hope. 'Where have you been since Mr Ludlow's death?'

'Mainly indoors. I was followed when I was with him. We heard the shouts; therefore, I was going to stay indoors until it concluded, but this, this is a young girl. I'm out with everybody, so it's not a problem. Large numbers. I didn't want to go about on my own, though.'

'Wouldn't you go along with friends?' asked Hope.

'What friends? I don't have friends. I have people I go swimming with. That's it.'

Hope thought for a moment, then she gave Perry a nod.

'We'll let you get back,' said Perry. 'Come on, I'll walk you over.'

Hope watched as Perry walked with the woman back to the group until she joined her team. Perry came back.

'Which one is Mrs Achterberg?' Hope asked.

'She's the one in that blue coat,' said Perry. 'Why do you ask?'

'She's been out searching with Gail and she hasn't said hello to her yet. Do you think that's . . .'

'That might be Gail. I don't think she's of the warmest of characters.'

'What do you think of her story, though?'

'The only thing with Gail that would make her a killer to me,' said Perry, 'is if she thought that Danny Poland was actually the person who killed Ludlow. But that's a far-fetched story. It doesn't make any sense. I think she's a woman seriously damaged. She looked for a dream and had it broken in front of her.'

'Do you think she's got nothing to do with it?'

'I didn't say that,' said Perry. 'I just said I didn't think she killed him. She might be involved. Those people shouting; Ludlow playing around. It all keeps coming back to me. There's too many people he could have been playing around with and who he could have offended.'

'There's always the business side too, isn't there?' said Hope. 'We still don't know what was said in discussions. Anything that was said, the only people that can report it are the franchisees. And if they killed him, they would not tell you bad things.'

'No, everybody got on well. But then again,' said Perry, 'as far as I can tell from Ross, this has been a success, this wild swimming. He was making money out of it.'

'Do you think he was a predator?' asked Hope.

'You mean, do I think he has done this before with other women?'

'Yes,' said Hope.

'It's hard to tell,' said Perry, 'having never met him when he was alive. But he certainly looks the part, doesn't he? He had that quiet dinner with Selina, which upset Carmen.

'You see, she could be our killer. She's also an excellent swimmer. Mrs Achterberg, she's not a swimmer at all. What happened with the boss and me, that couldn't have been her. She couldn't have been the one on the rocks diving in. She's not fit for it.'

'Where do we go from here?' asked Hope.

'I think we need a connection,' said Perry. 'We need to know who those two people were, shouting at Gail. We need to know who's after her.'

'Well,' said Hope, 'it makes sense that it might be Tabitha.'

'It does, but she's got no local connection. The boss was right when he talks about locals being the ones who would know the kids without actually having to know them. Locals could talk, ask questions, and come back with answers. They could formulate pictures of people in their head to go after without knowing them intimately. Tabitha doesn't work for that.'

'No,' said Hope, 'but she's the jealous girlfriend. If she knows this is what he's doing, why's she up here?'

'They'd spent a few days together and then he was off doing business. I guess it must be hard keeping up with him if he's travelling round.'

'Or,' said Hope, 'she's up to keep an eye on him.'

'Suppose,' said Perry.

'Let's follow the teams here a minute. I want to see something, want to clock our people.'

Perry led Hope off to where the search teams were walking. She'd seen Mrs Achterberg—already identified by Perry—and also Gail. The two of them were following their search coordinator and seemed to be genuinely getting on with it. Hope asked Perry to take her to the other team, so she could have a look at Mr Achterberg.

It took them ten minutes to find the other search team. When they did, Perry pointed him out.

'Big enough lad, isn't he?' said Perry.

'Older, but he's fairly fit, I think. Seems like he could do the swimming.'

'Strange he's not with his wife, though. I don't get that.'

'Where's Tabitha?' asked Hope.

'Not here,' said Perry. He walked up to the search coordinator in Achterberg's group. 'You had a woman helping you here. Tabitha. Tabby.'

'Oh, she's had to go. It's not unusual. You get people who can search for an hour or two. But she's had to go.'

'Did she seem all right?' asked Perry.

'Yes. Much as anyone. Working in a small team at the front there. The man is Achterberg. He's got a funny name, hasn't he?' said the guide. 'There was him, there was that woman there, Harriet, and there's Ella, Andy, and Tabby was in with them.'

'Thank you,' said Perry, walking back to Hope. 'She's gone. Gone back to her hotel room.'

'I'm getting cold, Perry,' said Hope. 'Let's get back to the station. Warm up a bit.'

'Why don't we take a spin out past Carmen and Selina's? See if they're there. See if any lights are on.'

'Why?' asked Hope.

'Just to get an idea of what they're doing. If they've gone to bed or whatever. We've got a search on here for one of the local girls.'

'You're clutching at straws,' said Hope.

'Maybe,' said Perry. 'I just feel like we're short of information. Just sort of . . .'

'Okay, we'll do it. But I'm staying in the car.'

Perry laughed. He got in the car and drove off towards Melvich. Hope took a deep breath and asked Perry, 'How are things at the moment?'

'What do you mean?' asked Perry.

'How are things? How's Ross?'

'Well, he's not getting at me as much as he used to. I think he's accepted the way I am, to some degree. Doesn't like it though. Well, that's his problem,' said Perry.

'Yes, it is,' said Hope. 'But what I'm saying is . . . how is he?'

'Not my place to say, is it, as a constable? He's my boss,' said Perry. 'I can't—'

'I want to help him, Perry,' said Hope. 'At the moment, he doesn't seem to fit in with the landscape. I was worried about bringing you in, the type of person you were, and yet you fit so well. At the moment, Ross doesn't seem to. I don't know. I'm asking you because you've got that experience. You've been around a bit, and you know people. You can read people. What's up with the man?'

'He doesn't enjoy working with you,' said Perry. 'He'd rather work with Macleod. Trouble is, Macleod has changed, I think, from what Ross used to know.'

'How do you mean?'

'I worked with Macleod down in Glasgow, and he's a changed person from then, yes, but he was always good at

181

finding people their role. But he doesn't want Ross in that role anymore. Ross used to cover off all the groundwork, from what I can gather. The sergeant should be there helping you, pushing the investigation. Do you remember being a sergeant?'

'Wasn't that long ago,' said Hope.

'I bet you pushed Macleod. I bet you had the odd ding with him.'

'I did.'

'When's Ross ever come at you? When's Ross told you that you've been doing wrong?' said Perry. 'When's Ross ever had a toe-to-toe?'

'He hasn't, really,' said Hope.

'No, he hasn't. He should be the one questioning you. He should be the one challenging what you're doing, in a nice way, because it'll make you better. I know why I'm here,' said Perry. 'I'm quirky, I think differently. A bit like Macleod, in that sense,' said Perry. 'But Ross? I don't think Ross knows why he's here anymore.'

'I wouldn't be good as a sergeant, not in a team like this,' said Perry. 'The trouble is, Ross isn't showing he's capable of it either. Yes, he can do the paperwork. Yes, he can do all that side of it. But as a sergeant, to an inspector, he needs to be your foil. The one that pushes you, like you pushed Macleod.'

'Thank you,' said Hope. 'And don't—'

'Don't what? Mention it?' said Perry. 'You really think I'm going to tell Ross, "Oh, by the way, the boss was looking for a bit of advice on you from me?" The man's not that fond of me to begin with.'

'No,' said Hope. 'He really isn't, is he?'

Chapter 21

'Sir, sir, I've got some things!'

Macleod rolled his neck, trying to loosen the stiff parts of it. 'I'm in the kitchen, Ross!' he shouted.

'Can you come to the laptop? I need to show you something.'

'You want coffee?' asked Macleod. There was no answer. It must have been good. Macleod poured himself coffee, anyway, and carried it through into the little office.

'What have you got for me?'

Ross was beaming now. Absolutely beaming. Macleod strode over to his desk, standing behind Ross as he pointed to the screen.

'I've been going back through the details of our potential owners. The Achterbergs, they seem to have moved up here from Wales. We've also got a problem. I can't find a daughter for the Achterbergs. When you were there originally, they talked about a daughter who was a wild swimmer. Yes?'

'Yes,' said Macleod. 'Abbey.'

'Well, Abbey's not about. There's no birth certificate,' said Ross. 'They don't have a daughter.'

'They don't have a daughter? There were photographs. Photographs of a girl, one who was swimming. Young though.

The photographs were young, but they said she grew up to be a—'

'I've checked into swimming records in the UK. There is no Achterberg, not there, none amongst all of it—'

'And you're saying there's no, what, record of a daughter at all?'

'None.'

Macleod put his hand down on the desk. 'Why do that though?' he said. 'Who is she then? Who's the girl in the photographs?'

'I don't know,' said Ross. 'I didn't see them.'

'Why would you have a photograph of a girl? Why would you . . .'

Macleod turned away for a moment.

'I've got more,' said Ross.

'Go on then,' said Macleod. 'Since you're on a roll.'

'I've been speaking to Europe about Selina and Carmen. They're new to the area. They admitted that much. But they've got history. History on the continent.'

'Really?'

'So, they've been together for a while. Several years from what I can see. They've got history on running schemes, and then leaving when the money dries up.'

'Schemes? What sort of schemes?'

'Clubs, societies, across all different walks of life. They basically run a fine line between a scam and a legitimate business. They take money off, skim it, from what I can see. They've never been around long enough in places to be nailed down and convicted. That's why they've been able to move about so easily. They're very shrewd. According to the contacts, Selina is the one that is shrewd. Carmen's the—well .

. . '

'Carmen's the what?' asked Macleod.

'Usually, some part of a scam has a good-looking figurehead. Carmen's the swimmer here at the moment. I don't know if she is. She fits the stereotype, but I don't know if she can even swim. I think she might be a fraud.'

'Would Ludlow have known that, though? He might have seen them as a fraud. He might have . . .'

'Bit much to kill over though,' said Ross. 'Attract attention. Why not just pack up and move on to the next scam if you got caught out like that? There's no history of murder around them. There're no killings in Europe, so I'm not sure that's the way things happen.'

'Question,' said Macleod. 'You said that some of these franchises were huge.'

'Yes.'

'So they could actually end up skimming off a lot of money. They could make a lot out of this before they ran, in a big way.'

'In a significant way,' said Ross. 'You will not run off with a million, but you could certainly keep going for several years.'

'So had Ludlow found out? Had he discovered something that could cause a conviction?'

'I don't think they're that daft,' said Ross.

'No,' said Macleod.

'But the big thing,' said Ross, 'is this. I'm looking up Gail Harmon. Gail's born in Wales, like the Achterbergs, but she lived in Suffolk before she came up here. She's changed her name, though.'

'Changed her name?'

'She got married and her husband died. When she got married, she changed her name. She used to be known as

Abigail Porter. And now she's become Gail Harmon.'

'Okay. That doesn't sound too unusual,' said Macleod.

'No, but I went to her birth certificate. Her birth certificate's only got her mother on it. No father mentioned.'

'She has said nothing about that to us, has she?'

'No.'

'I wonder why she's got no father,' said Macleod.

'Well, she has a father,' said Ross.

Macleod looked down at him incredulously.

'Well, I know that,' said Macleod, 'but not on the certificate. I wonder what happened to her mum. Ludlow was a hunger for her. Except Ludlow was aggressive to her, trying to push the issue, before she went out that night and had dinner with him. I wonder if there's any history with the father. I wonder if there's—'

'It's a bit of a stretch, isn't it?' said Ross.

'We're at a point of stretching, Ross. We haven't got anything. We've got nothing permanent, no proof. Find her mother. Find Abigail Porter's mum. I need to talk to her.'

He went to stride off, but he turned round. 'Thank you for that, Ross. It's good.'

Macleod strode back out to the kitchenette with his coffee. He stood there for a couple of minutes, then realised his feet were beginning to hurt. He thought about going out to the car, but it was cold outside. So, he wandered down the corridor and out to the front desk. There was a sergeant there, and Macleod nodded as he entered the small office. He sat down in his seat.

'Can I get anything for you, sir?'

'I've got my coffee. I should have brought you one,' said Macleod. 'And it's Seoras.'

'Of course, Seoras, sir.' Macleod smiled. They all did that.

'What's your name?' asked Macleod.

'Constable Angus Smith,' said the man, who looked like he was in his late fifties.

'Bit old for a constable,' he said.

'Bit old when I joined. But I managed. I'm really the desk duty. The other night shift's coming. Busy tonight with the search and that on.'

'I'm sure it is,' said Macleod. 'Can I ask you something?'

'Of course, Seoras,' he said.

'Community here. How long would it take you to know who's who? To have a rough idea.'

'Wouldn't be that hard if you're getting out and about.'

'Okay then. Who's Gail Harmon?' asked Macleod.

'Ah. Now, I do know who she is, but I've only known her recently because you've been investigating. Prior to that, no, I wouldn't have known her.'

'But she runs a group that goes swimming down at Fresco.'

'I don't really walk along the beach. Might have seen her shopping, I guess.'

'What about the Achterbergs? Mr and Mrs Achterberg—do you know them?'

'Oh yes, seen them about. He's quite the man, isn't he? Likes to organise, likes to think he is something. She's a lovely woman, though. She's been involved in quite a few community things. He's a bit more, well, a bit stuck up for my liking.'

'But they've been here a while now?'

'Not very long, really. This Gail Harmon's been here a long time and I've barely seen her,' said Angus.

'What about Selina Soto and Carmen Cabral?'

'Well, yeah, I know who they are. They haven't been here

a moment, but they were kind of the talk of the place, you know? You can imagine. Exotic. What's she, Brazilian?'

'Chilean,' said Macleod. 'The other one's Spanish.'

'Well, yes, I mean, they're down at the bay, Melvich. Been seen in the water. Word gets about when women like that swim, especially among the younger men. They also have been seen in a few of the pubs and that. A bit livelier than the others you spoke about.'

'Do you think they would know people in the community?'

'I don't know. Who are you thinking of?'

'Like the young lads that found the body,' said Macleod.

'Well, you think about it,' said Angus. 'The young lads will have noticed them. You would do at that age, wouldn't you?'

'Would they notice Gail Harmon?' said Macleod.

'Quite a shy woman. Boys wouldn't be looking for that, would they? They'd be looking at the Spanish woman. What's this all about anyway?' asked Angus, 'if I may.'

'Well,' said Macleod, 'keep this to yourself. Danny Poland's dead. How well would you know that Danny Poland was part of those other boys? The ones who found the body?'

'Well, I know that,' said Angus. 'A large part of the community would have known them as groups, even if you didn't know the names.'

'What if you'd just arrived? Would you?'

'You need to be here for a wee while.'

'But say you hadn't been here at all, maybe a week. Would you have clocked them going about together?'

'Unlikely. I mean, they were young lads. You'd have seen them at the school. But you'd have to be around the schools to do that, wouldn't you?' said Angus. 'They liked to hang about in the middle of the town. They weren't that notable, in that sense. They weren't bad lads. Jimbo had a rough time with his dad. But generally, you know, the schoolteachers and that would know them. People who've come in from the outside? No.'

'Thank you,' said Macleod. He continued to sit there, and Angus watched him for a moment, before saying, 'Is there anything else I can help you with?'

'No, you go ahead, whatever you're doing,' said Macleod. 'I'm just going to sit here, because it's nice and warm, and it's away from my sergeant. I need to let him work.'

'Right,' said Angus. He was soon answering phone calls, and Macleod sat in the chair with his feet stretched out in front of him.

So the Achterbergs had come up from Wales. Gail had also lived in Wales. Then she'd gone to Suffolk. Now she was up here, having changed her name from Abigail Porter, when she got married, to Gail Harmon. Birth certificate with a mother on it. No father. But if there's no father, why? What had happened? He didn't understand why she was a recluse, why she kept hidden away. But who then was after Ludlow?

Macleod stood up, stretched, and sat down again, causing Angus to throw a glance over. When he sat down again, he began thinking about the sea. He thought about being up on those rocks, about the person standing over him. They had been fit. They had been a swimmer, hadn't they? Was Carmen really a swimmer?

It was one thing to go into the water geared up and stand around prancing in it for a bit. It was another to swim through all that. Gail could swim through that. Who else could swim through it? Tabby? Did Tabby swim through it? Achterberg couldn't. But Tabby made no sense. Tabby was out of town.

189

Tabby wouldn't have known the boys. She couldn't have.

And then everything swung back to Gail. Or a potluck on Carmen. Carmen would have been a crime of passion. Carmen would have been killing Ludlow because he tried to hit it off with Selina. Macleod had seen those cases. It wasn't like Selina was angry at Carmen. It wasn't like she was in panic stations. They didn't look like people who had killed. But then again, many people didn't. Gail, however, she was reacting badly. Her story was changing.

But that could be because of her nature. The details fitted both ways with her, didn't they? Maybe she was panicking. A life of sadness, disappointment, tragedy. Or it could be she was covering up. Killing the man because he turned out not to be her dream. Her perfection.

If they could find Abigail Porter's mother, maybe, just maybe, they could get a different angle on Gail, one they could understand. Macleod stretched his feet again. Time was rolling on, and that was really bothering him. Somewhere out there, a sixteen-year-old girl was terrified and alone, or possibly very dead. He needed to find out soon.

Inside, something was gnawing at him. A voice of despair, a voice of sadness. Something told him it would be too late for Paula, and he couldn't help kicking himself for it.

That was the problem with being a policeman at a certain age. You were searching for someone and had to stay optimistic. You had to keep hopeful. But Macleod knew. He clenched his hand into a tight fist and gently tapped the chair he was on. He hoped he was wrong. But deep down, he knew he was right.

Chapter 22

Perry was at a bit of a loss. He'd gone out with Hope to put pressure on Gail Harmon. And having successfully done that, and achieved an explanation of her behaviour, Hope and he had returned to report to Macleod. After that, he wondered what to do. The search party was out, and he thought about joining them. Macleod, however, warned against that. That wasn't his function at the moment. His was to use his brain and dig up some evidence.

However, in the early hours of the morning, things seemed to have reached an impasse.

'Why don't you get some sleep?' said Hope to Perry.

'You're probably going to need more sleep than me. After all, you're looking after two—'

'I'm banning that, okay?' said Hope. 'I'm banning comments like that. I'm not looking after two. Well, yes, I am looking after two. But I'm looking after me. And I know what I'm capable of. And if I've got issues on that front, I will talk to Seoras and I will withdraw. It's not your job to keep an eye on me.'

'Sorry,' said Perry. He gave a gracious smile, but he was only trying to help. Hope needed to look after herself.

He thought about what she'd said, though. Previously around Susan, had he tried too hard? Did he care too much? That was part of his problem, but that was him. He did care. He wanted to help.

Perry stood out in the kitchenette, getting some space between Hope and himself. He could sit down at a desk, but he'd just look silly fidgeting. Out here, if somebody came in, maybe they'd see he was making a coffee.

He spied the flask on the side. It would hold maybe, what, three, four cups? He quickly boiled the kettle and, with some instant coffee, made up the flask and thought about Susan. She liked a drop of milk in hers, didn't she?

He put milk in the flask, put the top on, gave it a quick shake, and then went to find his large jacket that she'd given to him. That'd have been nice, hadn't it? A nice touch. He had been worried with Susan that he'd fallen so far from grace they were barely going to be friends, just mere colleagues. But she seemed to be warming back up to him. Not that she gave any sign she wanted anything more than that, but at least that was better than having chased her off completely.

He took the flask under one arm and marched off to find the search parties. He dropped by the base and asked exactly where Constable Cunningham was. It was then pointed out to him she was up towards the front.

At the moment, they'd worked out of the town and were searching towards some sea cliffs. Perry could see them in the distance, a myriad of torches, and quickly made his way up. He couldn't find Susan on arrival, but saw the party that had been Mr Achterberg's. Seeing some of the familiar faces of the group, he also recognised that Tabitha Green was now there, although Mr Achterberg seemed to have disappeared.

He looked around carefully, seeing if Susan was there, but she wasn't, and so turned to one of the other search parties, not that far away. When he got to their lights, he saw it was the party that had contained Mrs Achterberg and Gail Harmon. Gail was there, Mrs Achterberg wasn't.

There must have been a lot of coming and going with these search parties, he thought. Slowly he approached Gail, tapped her on the shoulder, and when she turned round, looking rather shocked, he said to her, 'Mrs Achterberg, did you see her go home?'

'Who?' asked Gail.

'Mrs Achterberg, with the sort of brown hair. Eh, older lady. I think she was in a green jacket. Well wrapped up. She's been with you most of the night.'

'Oh, her?' said Gail. 'Sorry, I don't know who she is. She's gone home.'

'Gone home?'

'Gone home,' said Gail. 'She said something about her husband. He was insisting they go. She was quite keen to stay. I think many people here are. There's a lot of chats between people about whether we're going to find her.'

'At least the sun will come up soon,' said Perry. 'You won't really see decent sunlight though until half seven.'

'It's only five at the moment,' said Gail. 'Is that everything? I need to get back to what I'm doing.'

Perry nodded and watched as the woman turned back, shining her torch here and there and stepping through the fields. Perry looked around, still trying to find Susan. When he spotted her, she was marching across with another group, but she stopped and sat down on a wall.

She was reaching down, feeling around her leg, as Perry

walked up to her.

'You okay?'

'Not really,' said Susan. 'It's beginning to bug me now. I think it's the cold. Been a long time on it.'

'Take a seat for a bit. You're not actually searching with them, are you?'

'No,' she said. 'I'm just trying to do what I can. Otherwise, I'm just standing by. I know I'm the liaison, but really, they can come and find me. It takes two minutes if they find anything. They talk to me. I've got a radio here,' she said, pulling out a walkie-talkie. 'Sit down, Perry.'

Perry put the flask on the wall, undid the top, taking one cup off the top. He poured a coffee and gave it to Susan.

'Thanks Perry,' she said. 'You're a lifesaver, you know that.' She sipped her coffee. 'Stay a moment,' she said.

Perry smiled as he sat beside her. 'Look,' she said. 'I know things were awkward between us there for a while. I just needed my own space. I know you—'

'It's okay,' said Perry. 'You don't have to explain. I'm just glad that we . . . well, we're on more of an even keel.'

'I really appreciate you,' she said. 'You saved me. You saved my leg. The other one. I would've been crushed in there. And you got me out. But I was scared. You suddenly were there all the time, helping, caring. And my feelings were awkward.'

'I guess so,' said Perry.

'I saw you as a friend. At least, I made myself see you as a friend because I was so all over the place. That's what I needed. Now, well . . . this is pathetic. We need to get on. I need to keep going. What I'm saying is, don't be a stranger. I'm not saying I'm wanting anything else. I'm just saying, be Perry around me. Don't tread on eggshells. This here, where you've just brought the coffee, is great.'

'Okay,' said Perry. 'I'll do my best.'

'You're still off the fags, I see,' she said.

'You don't like them, do you? Cigarette smokers.'

'You stank. Did you know that? Your clothes stank,' she said. 'You're better without them. But you need to take care of yourself, too. Like running around in suit jackets in this weather. You're warm now, at least, with your big fluorescent coat.' Susan laughed, but then suddenly winced.

'What's up?' asked Perry.

'It's the leg, Perry. It's just the interface between what's me and what's the new bit. I've been on it a lot. I keep wanting to rub it, but I can't feel anything. Cold inside. This coffee's helping, but I probably should get indoors soon. But I don't want to leave this, do I?'

'Which bit's not feeling right?' said Perry. He left the flask on the wall and knelt down in front of Susan. She lifted her prosthetic up and started to pull up the trouser leg of her waterproof.

'Here,' said Perry.

Perry pushed the trouser back and saw the attachment. 'Take it off,' she said. 'Then work around the stump and try to put a bit of feeling back into it.'

Susan sat while Perry worked as best he could, trying to warm her leg up. After five minutes, he reattached her prosthetic and re-rolled down the trouser leg and waterproof.

'Thank you,' she said.

'Any better?' he asked.

'If I said it was wonderful, I'd be lying. It's better than it was.'

'Do you want to get warm for an hour? I can cover this.'

'No,' she said. 'I need to be here. We're heading down

towards the coast now.'

'Why are you heading down there now?' asked Perry. 'I thought they'd covered that before.'

'The tide was in. We couldn't get down on the bottom cliffs. Also, we're going to get some sort of light soon. You don't want to walk around those cliffs in the dark. You and Seoras near came a cropper on them in the daylight.'

'That's true,' said Perry.

'Seoras said you saved him, flung yourself into the battle.'

'I couldn't keep up with him. You know that, Susan? I couldn't keep up with him. I was half knackered. We got there, the old man . . . well, she put him on the floor. I thought she was going to do him in. I just jumped over. Hit her with what I had. ME! Flung myself at her. We got lucky. It chased her off.'

'That's quite something,' said Susan.

'Don't,' said Perry. 'You're not doing that to me.'

'You know, Hope asked me what I saw in you.' Perry saw Susan gazing at his eyes, her face deadly serious.

'She did?'

'Yes. She asked me what I saw in you. And that's what I see in you. At times you're just selfless. Completely selfless. It's one of your best features. You know that.' Perry felt himself blushing. 'Don't change,' she said. 'Never change from that.'

Susan jumped up onto her legs. 'They're getting ahead of us. Come on, let's follow them down to the cliff. Unless you're going off to get some sleep.'

'I'm actually at a loss. You know that?' said Perry. 'I'm at a blooming loss. I've been thinking things through and can't get my head round it. I can't clock what's happening. Two people dead. Why? Who's doing it? Who's the local involved?'

'Well, it's more your field than mine. I'm just trying to focus on this.'

'I see Achterberg went home. Both of them.'

'Yes. He went off, and then Tabitha turned up. Oh, maybe a half hour later.'

'Really?' said Perry. 'Interesting. You know that Mrs Achterberg and Gail don't know each other.'

'So I hear. Anyway, come on.'

The two of them plodded on in the dark with their torches, catching up with the groups that were now moving down to the sea cliffs. One group was far ahead. As Perry and Susan reached the top of the cliffs, looking out in the dim twilight of the sky and the lapping sea far below, they could see the group was right at the water's edge.

'What have they gone down there for?' asked Perry.

Susan consulted her map. 'There's a sea cave there. It's one of those that is not big but apparently you can get inside it. You can lie down in it.'

'Right,' said Perry.

There was a shout from below. The walkie-talkie burst into life.

'DC Cunningham, this is base.'

'Base, Cunningham,' replied Susan.

'Number three search party's found something right down on the coast. I can give you coordinates.'

'I think I see them from the top of the cliffs,' said Cunningham. 'I'll join them now.'

Carefully, Susan and Perry made their way down the cliffs, following the trail that gave the easiest descent. It took a good five minutes to get down to the cave where lights were being waved at them. On arrival, the search leader of that party gave a look that told Susan all she needed to know.

'We found some clothes on the way down,' he said. 'They're just there. I've got somebody standing by them, told them not to touch them.'

'We'll get our forensic officer down immediately,' said Susan, and went to turn.

'No, that's why I called you down. I would have called you with the radio otherwise and said it. We found her.'

'And?' said Susan.

The man shook his head. 'She's not in a good way.'

'Meaning?'

'If you come down, you can just about get round and inside the cave. I was the one who found her, and I haven't sent anybody else in. Haven't told them what I've seen. I don't think anybody else should go in there until your forensic officer does. But I would say they should hurry. The tide's gone down, but it won't stay. She's maybe got two, three hours to get in there safely.'

'Very good,' said Susan. She walked past the man and looked at the climb round the cliff.

'Perry,' she said, 'I'm not sure I'll get in there easily. I don't want to disturb anything. Can you get in?'

Perry looked at it. 'Sure,' he said. There was a narrow ledge round, and he was sure he could walk round it.

The search leader turned to him and said, 'I've got some rope. Probably best if I attach you to me and some of the rest of us. That way, if you have a slip, you will not disappear out into the sea.'

Perry nodded as the man clicked the gear round him. Perry had taken a head torch off the leader, leaving his hands free to cling to the rocks. The surface was slippery as he worked

CHAPTER 22

his way inside the cave, which was dark. He switched on the head torch. Initially, the torch just showed moist rock here and there. Then Perry turned his head left.

He nearly fell backwards as a face looked at him. It was Paula. He'd seen the face in pictures, but not like this. She was battered, bruised. Her body was also naked. Perry didn't touch it, but he moved himself across the rock so that he could have a full look at her body. From where he was, he could see bruising, not just on her face, but around intimate parts, too. Her arms also had bruises. The ribs looked caved in. Poor girl looked like she'd been battered. Maybe she'd been interfered with as well. His heart sank.

Beside the body, Perry could see some papers, and had to lift himself up, holding a brace position above her legs, to see what was behind her. There were photographs. He saw Selina, Carmen, Mrs Achterberg, and Gail. All photos of their meetings with Stephen Ludlow. There were specifically lots about Gail. Perry didn't want to lift them or touch them. But he took out his phone and snapped photographs of some of them.

He then photographed the body as best he could, before making his way back out of the cave. As he emerged, his head torch lit up the face of Susan Cunningham.

'Don't go in,' he said. 'We need Jona quickly. Quick as we can. I need to talk to Macleod as well. There are photographs in there,' he said. 'Photographs of Ludlow meeting different women. The women from the franchises.'

'And Paula?'

Perry clenched his fist. 'Poor girl,' he said. 'Poor, poor girl.'

Chapter 23

Jona Nakamura was stretched to the limit. Why did they keep leaving bodies in sea caves? Why was evidence so hard to get hold of? She had raced down to the scene with her team and her photographer had been inside, capturing every detail. The body was quickly put into a bag and removed once the entire area had been photographed.

They were working as quickly as they could to preserve what evidence there was. Photographs and other items around the body were collected, sealed away, and brought out of the cave. Jona Nakamura was also consulting with the Coastguard, working out how high the tide would have been.

She had come back out of the cave, and was standing with a pad of paper, drawing various levels to work out just where the sea had been inside the cave.

'Jona,' said a voice. The morning was now just about breaking, the path down to the sea cave no less treacherous, just more visible. But she recognised the fedora that was at the top of the cliffs. Macleod was wrapped up in his long coat, scarf around his neck, and beside him, in a bobble hat, was a six-foot woman.

'Hope!' cried Jona. 'Well, it's nice to see a happier face for once.'

She watched Macleod about to descend and waved at him. 'Don't,' she said. 'There's nothing to see. I'll come up to you. I'll show you the photographs up top. You won't get into the cave. The water's rising now.'

Jona made her way up, with Macleod watching her the whole way up. He was clearly desperate for information.

'You okay?' he asked.

Jona took a deep breath. 'Yes,' she said. 'I will be. If I was you, I'd check Perry too. That wasn't nice. Really wasn't nice.'

'What can you tell me?'

'She was beaten, she was sexually assaulted, struck in a manner that would suggest someone with a perversion. She was hit in places you shouldn't be hit. The bruising wasn't from simply a sexual encounter. It was . . . yeah. I need to get back and write it all up and take a proper look.'

'How long's she been dead?' asked Macleod.

'Not very. The bruising that's there is the more the immediate sort. Probably happened to her over the last day or so. But she's been dead not long. She's also not been in that cave very long.'

'What makes you say that?' asked Macleod.

'Well, the tide would have come up, and she'd have floated on it. And then she'd have been taken out there,' said Jona, pointing to the sea. 'She has been put in there since the tide fell down last. You've maybe got a six-hour-or-less window, at most.'

'So somebody's put her in there. She wasn't killed in there.'

'Serrated blade in the back. Just like Ludlow.'

'Okay. Where's your wagon?' asked Macleod. 'I want to ask some things but not out here.'

Jona nodded, pulling back her coverall, and shook her hair, wrapped up in a ponytail.

'Let's go get a coffee,' said Jona. 'I need a coffee.'

They made their way over to the forensic wagon. Stepping into the back, Jona went to do the coffees. Macleod told her no, and to sit down, and told Hope to sit with her. They did so while Macleod put the kettle on. A few minutes later, he'd made coffee, and had it in front of Jona, who gripped it tightly.

'When you say,' Macleod said, 'that she was sexually abused and then hit in places that you wouldn't hit people, was it a man that sexually abused her?'

Jona nodded. 'Penetrative sex,' she said.

'I'm just a little confused,' said Macleod. 'I was chasing a woman. Definitely a woman. I know sometimes, and certainly recently, we had people who were androgynous. But that figure I saw was not androgynous.'

'It'll be a reasonably powerful man. She's a sixteen-year-old girl, but she seems reasonably strong. If someone is violating you in that way, quite often you'll strike out hard for all your worth. To hold somebody in that position, to carry out your attack, takes a bit of strength.'

'And the serrated blade? You believe it's the same one?' asked Macleod.

'I can't know that yet,' said Jona. 'Possibility. Strong possibility. The wound looks about the same size. I didn't have time to look that closely. We needed to get the body out of there. We had no time frame in which to do proper investigations in situ.'

'Understood,' said Macleod. 'The photographs are . . . ?'

'Over there,' said Jona, pointing to the side of the wagon. Macleod went over with Hope and looked at each one in turn.

'It's all the women with Ludlow,' said Macleod. 'There's no Mr Achterberg.'

'Who took these? Somebody's taken them from a distance?' asked Hope.

'Mr Achterberg isn't in any of them,' said Macleod. 'The one of Mrs Achterberg seems to be taken . . . well, from where? If he was taking a photograph of Ludlow and her, he wouldn't take it from a distance. He would take it right there in front of him. He's part of the meetings, isn't he?'

'That's what you told me,' said Hope. 'I wasn't here for the interviews.'

'He was,' said Macleod. 'Yet that photograph of Mrs Achterberg is taken from a distance. Mr Achterberg isn't in any of the photographs. That indicates that he took that picture of Mrs Achterberg, because he doesn't talk about being away from her.'

'And if he was there all the time, it would be very hard to shoot these photographs. Why would he shoot photographs of just Mrs Achterberg and Ludlow?' asked Hope.

'Exactly,' said Macleod. 'Ross has discovered that the Achterbergs used to be down in Wales. They said they had a daughter who was into competitive swimming. They have no child on record by birth certificate.'

'Well, that's suspicious. Why would they tell you a lie like that, though?' asked Jona.

'It wasn't just a lie,' said Macleod. 'It was a photograph of a girl.'

'What are you thinking?' asked Hope. 'Achterberg is, well, suspicious to say the least.'

'He's got a military background. He's strong enough and could contain someone, hold them prisoner. From training,

203

he would know how to do these things,' said Macleod. 'But why? He said he had to warn Ludlow off with his wife. But warn him off and then just kill him? He never did much else. Mrs Achterberg didn't even say much about it. It sounded like the man was a flirt. They then had to just humour him, but lay the line down.

'But what about the person who saw Gail?' continued Macleod. 'Male voice. And a female voice in the crowd. But why? It just seems too much that he would do something like that because somebody was slightly flirtatious with his wife. They were trying to get a business together. It just makes little sense.'

There was a knock at the door. Susan Cunningham entered. 'I'm sending everyone home. What do you want me to do once I've got that done?'

'Give them all my thanks,' said Macleod, 'and then join us. You and Perry.'

Susan left the wagon, and as Macleod was about to begin again, talking through the photographs, the door was knocked for a second time.

'Come in,' said Macleod. Ross entered, walking directly to Macleod.

'I got a photo of Abigail Porter's mother,' he said. 'This is a photo of her and her child.' Macleod stared at it. 'She wouldn't tell me much about the father. Just said that Abigail has no father. I pushed her to say what happened, and she, well, she eventually admitted it—'

'She was raped,' said Macleod suddenly.

'Yes, she was.'

Macleod took Ross's phone, staring at it carefully. 'Hope,' said Macleod, 'look at this. This photograph, Abigail Porter's mum, Abi . . . Abi . . . the Achterberg photo has their Abi in it. We've been looking at the same Abi. We have seen Abi the whole time. Gail Harmon is Abi. That's her as a child. On the phone here, Ross's phone. That's the same girl who was in the photograph at the Achterbergs. I'm sure of it.'

'So what?' said Hope.

'Gail Harmon is Achterbergs' daughter. Two voices,' said Ross. 'Husband and wife.'

'Husband and wife,' said Macleod. 'Maybe. They also disappeared from the search. Jona said there wouldn't have been a lot of time to get that body in.'

'But what about the woman? The woman who attacked Jimbo?' asked Hope.

'Maybe Mrs Achterberg is more of a swimmer than she's letting on,' said Ross.

'I don't know about that,' said Macleod. 'But we need to go, Hope. We need to get to the Achterbergs.' Macleod grabbed his hat, Hope standing up when he began to race off.

'Get these photographs, that explanation to the rest of the team, Ross,' said Macleod, before leaving. 'Jona, I need your team to follow. You're going to want DNA, whatever we can grab off him. I need to search his house, find out where they've kept her.'

Hope drove Macleod, hammering along the short distance to the Achterberg house. Macleod sat silently, but his hands were gripped tight, knuckles white.

Macleod jumped out of the car, thundered on the door, and rang the doorbell. He made as much noise as he could. It took a moment before he saw a light come on at the top of the house and then heard footsteps on the stairs. The door opened to reveal Mrs Achterberg in her dressing gown.

'Where is your husband, please?' asked Macleod.

'Alec?'

'Is he up in bed with you?' asked Hope.

'No, no. I came back—had to get to sleep. I'm exhausted. He went out to the shed. Said he couldn't sleep. Said he needed to do something.'

'With me,' said Macleod to Hope. The two of them tore around the side of the building to where they saw the large barn at the back. Macleod rapped on it.

'Mr Achterberg? Alec? Are you in there?'

There were no lights on inside, and Macleod slowly opened the door. He made his way along the wall, fumbling desperately for a switch. Looking into the interior, he couldn't see anything, so dark was the morning. And then he found the switch. Flicking it on, he turned to look into the middle of the room.

About two feet above the floor, was a set of feet. They were attached to Alec Achterberg. His body wasn't swinging, but hanging motionless, the neck held up by a rope attached to the ceiling around a beam. Macleod saw Hope race forward, grabbing his legs, pushing him upright.

As Macleod tore across the room, he saw where the rope had been tied, quickly fumbling with it, desperately trying to release Mr Achterberg. He saw the rope come clear, and Hope laid the man down on the ground. She reached down for his neck.

'No pulse,' she said. 'Nothing. Beginning CPR.'

It was another twenty minutes before Jona arrived, followed three minutes later by an ambulance. By the time the paramedics had reached the body, Jona had declared the man dead.

Macleod stood outside the barn. He could hear the wailing of Mrs Achterberg on her front doorstep. Perry had arrived and was dealing with the woman, along with Susan Cunningham. Macleod was standing with Hope. Jona emerged from the barn.

'How long's he been dead?' asked Macleod.

'Couple of hours?' offered Jona.

'He left the search,' said Macleod. 'They've come home. Couple of hours takes in that. So, he could have been killed not long after he got home.'

'It's my best guess,' said Jona. 'What you didn't notice was that up his back, a serrated blade has been driven in several times.'

'Several times?' said Macleod.

'Several times.'

'So what? Did he hang himself and then knife himself?'

'To hang yourself is hard enough. To actually stab yourself while hung up there seems like a nigh on impossibility. And also, the knife would have dropped,' said Jona. 'Somebody killed him beforehand. The blade looks like it could be the same. Certainly the same type of weapon.'

'But,' said Macleod, 'you said he was stabbed several times. Your previous victims were stabbed once.'

'By somebody who knew what they were doing,' said Jona. 'This person didn't. The knife is wielded erratically. They were lucky to hit the right organs to finish him. This person is somebody else.'

Just when Macleod thought his night's work was done, something else had reared its head. Who though? Who did it? Macleod thought hard. The entire picture was there. He just needed to see it.

Chapter 24

Hope jumped in the car, Macleod beside her. They weren't that far away. All they had to do was to get to Thurso.

'And we're going to Tabitha Green because?' asked Hope.

'Because there's two of them. The reason we couldn't understand it is because there wasn't a husband-wife combination. It wasn't two women. There were two of them. The woman who went into the sea when Perry and I chased her—she is a swimmer. She's a proper swimmer. But it was a man who killed and killed well. Military background.'

'Still not with it,' said Hope.

'Trust me,' said Macleod. He called the others, telling them to follow him, but Hope and he were already well ahead, pulling up at the hotel. Macleod strode into the front desk. There were people now having breakfast, and he asked where Tabitha Green was, and if she had checked out.

The woman examined her records. 'No.' Macleod, asked what time she had last entered her room.

'Six o'clock-ish. Half six, something like that. Hang on.' The woman scanned down the screen. 'Yes, half-past six this morning.'

CHAPTER 24

That was rather long, thought Macleod. *But the Achterbergs had left, so Tabby hadn't come to the hotel. The times were close and Tabby could argue she came straight here. It was tight given the prolonged nature of the end, people hanging around while things were confirmed. When was the search concluded? He checked the time. She could have got over to the Achterbergs, couldn't she? Surely.*

Macleod took the lift up, while Hope climbed up the flights of stairs, both arriving together outside Tabby Green's room. Macleod knocked on the door once, then twice. The door opened up and Tabby Green was standing in what looked to Macleod like a long T-shirt.

'Detective Chief Inspector,' she said.

'And Detective Inspector McGrath,' said Macleod.

'I'm trying to get some sleep. We've been out all night.'

'Indeed,' said Macleod. 'I need to ask you something. Before you joined the search, and then after it was called off, what did you do?'

'I didn't hear about the search beforehand. I'd been out walking.'

'Walking,' said Macleod. 'At what time?'

'It was late at night, I admit that. Not been sleeping easy since what happened to Stephen. Hard to sleep. Hard to . . .'

'Do you have access to photographs? Some sort of large camera?'

The woman shook her head. Macleod was inclined to believe her.

'Are you aware that Stephen had slept with someone before his death?'

'Stephen was always a rather independent person,' said Tabby.

209

'You left the search; what did you do?' asked Macleod.

'Came here.' said Tabby.

'And what time was that at?'

'I can't say exactly. I was tired. I was . . .'

'Half-past six,' said Macleod. 'You left the search. Where did you go?'

'I got out, drove for a bit.'

'And why?' asked Macleod.

'Because, well, it's hard to get back to sleep, isn't it? I mean, we just found her. Get that image out of your head; drive around for a bit. That's what I was trying to do.'

'Where's your car?' asked Macleod.

'It's down in the car park.' She was starting to look more anxious.

'Have you left the hotel at all since you got back?'

'No,' she said.

'Put some clothes on. Detective Inspector McGrath will stay here by the door. I'll step outside. And then I want you to take us down and show us your car. Don't be long, please.'

He gave Hope a nod. She still looked a little bemused as Macleod stepped outside. Five minutes later, they made their way down to the car park.

'Open the boot for me,' said Macleod. Tabby duly did so and Macleod saw a wetsuit inside. It was damp. 'Why have you got that?' he asked.

'There's always a wetsuit in my car.'

'And it's damp,' said Macleod. 'When was the last time you went for a swim in it?'

'Earlier on today. It's what I do. I'm a swimmer,' said Tabby. 'Nothing unusual about that.'

Macleod looked elsewhere in the boot. There was a flash-

210

light. There were wet clothes as well.

'From the search,' said Tabby. 'This hotel doesn't do laundry. I was going to take it into town tomorrow. It seemed the best bet. And having found the girl, I was probably going to make my way home. Was going to phone you to tell you.'

Macleod closed the boot down. 'What do you know of Mr Achterberg?'

'He's one of the hopeful franchisees, isn't he? I gave you that information. Stephen mentioned him during those last few days.'

'Did you see him tonight?'

'I don't know what you mean. Where?'

'At the search—did you see Mr Achterberg?'

'I don't know what he looks like.'

'He was very keen to get into your group tonight. In fact, left his wife to do so.' Macleod saw the slightest of flinches. 'But then, he's there and you're not. And then after that, he's gone and you're there.'

'What has this to do with me?' Tabby blurted.

'Yourself and Mr Achterberg. Does he do photographs?'

'How do you mean?'

'We found photographs beside the body. Why would there be any need for these photographs? What use would Achterberg have for these photographs?'

'Because he was being a rat. Stephen was being a rat. I don't know. Was Mr Achterberg somehow linked in with one of them?'

'Mr Achterberg is Gail Harmon's father. At least, he raped her mother.'

And there it was. There was the flinch. The shock. The incomprehension. To anybody that didn't really know Achterberg, you wouldn't have thought twice. But Tabby was showing genuine shock, not just that feeling of rather unpleasantness about someone you didn't know. This was someone she'd been close to, Macleod was sure of it.

'Had you seen Mr Achterberg before coming here?'

'No.'

'But you met him, didn't you? You met him outside Gail Harmon's house. Because you were tailing Stephen.'

'I don't know what you're talking about.'

'Yes, you do. You were tailing him,' said Macleod.

'I was out helping. Don't know who the man is.'

'No, but your timings are interesting. Very interesting. What did he do?' asked Macleod. 'Or did you convince him? Why are you up here? Why would you come to a hotel and then not go with Stephen?'

'I told you I came up here with him. We had a bit of time together and then he was off doing business.'

'You never wanted to be part of that business?' asked Hope. 'Never wanted to go along? You're a swimmer. He was in everyday swimming with people. Alternative place to go swimming.'

'One bit of sea's like the other,' said Tabby.

'You're a sea swimmer,' said Macleod. 'I'm finding that hard to believe. Disappeared from the search. Achterberg had already gone. He's dead now. Killed with the same blade we think has killed everyone else. The only problem is, the blade wasn't there, and it hadn't been wielded into his back in a professional way. You see, I think Mr Achterberg killed Stephen Ludlow. Stephen was killed quickly, almost effortlessly, professionally. But I chased down a woman when she was chasing after one of our witnesses. Except nobody quite knew what the witnesses saw.

'Although the boys said to me that different people were seen at the same time. Cars were going past their houses. Maybe you just got lucky with Jimbo being on his own. Or maybe somebody could have found that out for you. Maybe you were a partnership.'

'Inspector, I have no idea what you're talking about. I've kept myself to myself,' she said. 'You've come; you've searched my car. Now, is there anything else?'

'I've looked in your boot,' said Macleod. 'I haven't searched your car. Maybe I'll get a warrant for that. Maybe I'll see what else I can dig up. Don't leave town,' said Macleod.

He went downstairs with Hope, out to the car. When they left the car park, he told her to pull up just up the street.

'You're off to find more evidence?'

'No,' said Macleod. 'Time to wait. If the car's the problem, I've told her I'm coming back for it. She'll leave very shortly, because if she leaves and dumps the evidence and comes back, we don't find that evidence to say it's her. I've got nothing concrete against her, but if she drives off here with evidence, we can stop her and search for it.'

It took ten minutes before Tabby Green's car pulled out of the car park, approximately one hundred yards down the road. Hope pulled up alongside her and told her to pull in. Macleod stepped out and asked her to open the boot. Inside was the wetsuit.

'You're harassing me now,' she said. 'There you go. It's still the wetsuit, the torch, and the damp clothes. I told you I have to lift these out and get them laundered. That's where I'm away to.'

'You accused me of waking you up a half hour ago, and now

213

you're instantly racing off to a laundry,' said Macleod.

'Look, you can check it all, open the doors of the car,' Tabby Green told Macleod. 'Have a proper look, pull down the glove compartment, look in the well of the driver's seat, underneath the seats, wherever you want. Have a look.'

Macleod pulled out some gloves, putting them on his hands. 'Open the boot again,' he said, Tabby having just closed it. Tabby opened it up. Macleod reached down the inside, and found two tabs that pulled up the floor of the boot. Underneath the floor was the spare wheel. Inside the spare wheel compartment were photos, some bloody garments, a serrated blade.

'If you can step away, please,' said Macleod. Hope took Tabby Green off to one side to read her rights.

Macleod looked down at the bloody mess left inside the wheel compartment. He picked up the phone, calling for Jona and for the rest of the team to arrive. Ten minutes later, a police car was taking Tabby Green off to be held for questioning, and a forensic wagon pulled up. Macleod stood aloof as his team got about their business.

Jona was bagging and tagging. Shortly the rest of the team gave him an update from investigations at the Achterbergs. After a moment, he sat down on the cold ground, his back up against a wall. Hope knelt down beside him.

'Are you okay?' she said.

Macleod shook his head. 'No. That girl,' he said. 'What he did to that girl.'

Hope sat down beside him and put her arm around Macleod. 'Yes,' she said. 'We didn't get there in time.'

'No,' Macleod said. 'I did not.'

Chapter 25

Macleod sat in the small interview room, Hope beside him, staring at Tabby Green. She had been crying intermittently. But recently, she'd come round to just staring at the wall.

'You clearly entered into a deal with him, some sort of effort, and yet you killed him. Why?' asked Macleod.

'Because, well, he killed my Stephen.'

'Did you not help in that?' asked Macleod.

'I placed Stephen where I thought you wouldn't find him. Until those boys went. I only just about got away from them.'

'In what way?' asked Macleod.

'When they entered, I was in the cave. I had just put Stephen up and I went under the water. I actually thought they'd seen me. Convinced of it.'

'But you obviously swum out without them seeing you.'

'We didn't know that.'

'But why were you planting his body there? You were obviously annoyed at his playing around.'

'Stephen had been making a fool of me for so long. I came up here to follow Stephen about, to see what he was doing. I was watching him when he saw Achterberg the first day.

215

'When he did that, I saw him with Mrs Achterberg. He was flirting. She wasn't responding. She wasn't interested. But he clearly was having an impact. I saw Mr Achterberg taking photographs. The next day, he was out seeing Gail Harmon. I followed him there as well. We both followed them out to the coffee shop. It was obscene. He was all over. Unlike the day before with Mrs Achterberg, he was losing it. I could tell he wanted her. I used to think that it was just me with him that drove him like that. It was a woman. Any woman could get him into that feverish state.

'That I was up here with him, I was barely ten miles away and he was doing this. It angered me. I saw him there about to go up to her flat and I shouted at him. He escaped. He tore off. But I saw Achterberg behind me taking photographs.

'So I approached him. We obviously had a common issue. I asked him what his problem was, why he was taking these photographs and he said that he was worried that Gail would be compromised. I asked him why that bothered him, and he said that Gail was a lovely person and shouldn't be taken in by someone like that. He knew what he was like after talking to his wife, so he said he would follow him that night.

'It was the next day when Achterberg told me Stephen had sex with her. He'd stayed the night. We traced him over to Carmen and Selina's there. He flirted, but they weren't having it. And that night, too, Carmen was obviously angry, but he didn't get what he wanted.

'He'd actually cheated on me. And Achterberg was raging. So we decided we would sort him out. I convinced Achterberg that he could kill him. What I didn't understand was how easily the man would do it. He intercepted him at some point, I don't know where. Put a knife in him and the next thing he presented him to me. Achterberg had got rid of the clothes and Stephen was naked. So, I put him into the cave.

'He wouldn't be found. He'd be missing for so long and never surface from the water because he was jammed into the cave. And those boys went in. That was our downfall. If those boys hadn't gone in, that cave would have been empty for years. He would have been stowed up there.'

'You could have just dumped him in the sea,' said Macleod.

'Then he would have been found dead and there would have been questions. The sea returns you eventually, especially close to the coast. I negated that risk. Achterberg swore the cave would never be used. Looking back, it was a terrible choice, but Achterberg had never been in it. He talks about sea swimming, but he's not a proper swimmer. When I got to the cave, I realised it might not be the best place, and then I got interrupted by the boys. Afterwards, I said to Achterberg that the boys had interrupted me.

'He got obsessive about whether or not they had seen anyone. I wasn't sure. I couldn't say they hadn't. He did some investigating, and he came up with the name of Danny Poland as one of the boys. We followed some of the rest of them, too. Danny Poland was in their group, according to Achterberg. So, we followed him. He went to the jewellery shop. That's when we saw him with Paula.

'Did Paula know? Had he told her? Achterberg got angry. I said I would try to get hold of one of them. I was all for capturing him, but you came on my tail. The one they called Jimbo. I probably would have killed him if you hadn't showed up. Thrown him off the rocks to drown or be smashed on them. So he couldn't speak, anyway. Whether he had seen anything, it was irrelevant when he was silent.

'Achterberg drove a lot of that. I wasn't keen, but neither was I keen to get caught. Achterberg, however, got more agitated. More angry. He seemed to lose it, thinking he was going to be caught. Said it would make him look bad.'

'Gail Harmon is Achterberg's daughter,' said Macleod. 'He raped her mother. She was born and her mother obviously had nothing to do with him, but he found where she was. That's why he moved up here with his new wife. Mrs Achterberg knew nothing about it.'

'So he set up a swim centre just to be near.'

'That's right,' said Macleod. 'That was why he didn't want the cover blown.'

'He gave me Danny Poland's body. I received the body quickly. But the girl, he grabbed the girl, and kept her. I didn't understand why at first. He was holding her. It was in a shed a little way off, not far from his house. Well, I said that it'd look bad for him if we didn't turn up on the search. So I said we'd swap over. I wasn't there at the start—he was and then I came along after and he would go back to her.

'We were trying to see if she knew anything. At least that was my plan. He wanted her alive for a while. Wanted to understand if he had to go for any more of them, he said. By that time when I went back, after he'd been with her, I understood exactly what he wanted her for. She was a mess. He had, well . . . you saw her. I wanted no more to do with him at that point.

'And I wanted to punish him. I took her clothes, planted them down by the rocks, planted her inside the cave, and came back to the search. But not before I'd called him, told him we had a problem. He needed to come back to his house. Said I'd meet him outside in his shed. He entered in the dark. I knew he had a military background, but he wasn't expecting what I did. He wasn't ready. I knifed him as soon as he stepped inside. Quickly, rapidly. I must have hit something right, because he died pretty quick. And I strung him up then.'

'Why string him up?'

'I guess I wanted to make it look like suicide.'

'Hard to knife yourself in the back for suicide.'

'Maybe, but I wasn't thinking straight at that point,' said Tabby. 'I couldn't have overpowered him easily. I needed to work quick. He'd shown me the blade he'd used. He'd shown me how quick he'd been with it. And the blade was there for me to use with Paula, if she got out of hand. But you cottoned on to it, didn't you?' said Tabby.

'There were too many things crossing over,' said Macleod. 'There had to be two people at work. Mrs Achterberg wasn't in the right shape for the woman who'd attacked me. She couldn't have done the things that had been done, putting her in the cave. She wasn't the woman we were looking for. Gail Harmon is a mess of a figure.

'Carmen, for all that she was angry, was no killer. And, the only person who had been slept with was Gail Harmon. So what was the offence? To see you as someone offended is quite easy. You could have been the woman that shouted. Gail didn't tell us that at first. If she had kept quiet about that, you'd have been clear.

'Instead, she did. She said there was a man's voice, too. And that's where I got confused. You had somebody with you. A private detective wouldn't cry out like that. Gail didn't know who it was. Of course she didn't. She was the genuine frightened figure. We had nothing on Achterberg's past. We didn't understand the animal he was.'

'But that wasn't my fault,' said Tabby. 'Not my fault at all. What he did. All of that, I'm not to blame. Stephen was cheating on me. I just wanted him out of the way.'

'You set in motion events that allowed that man to do what he did to young Paula,' said Macleod. 'I hope they throw the book at you. I hope they lock you away for a long time. To have no remorse over that. You'll be taken down to Inverness. There'll be more interviews.'

He stood up, closed the interview, and left the room with Hope. Macleod walked back to their little room where his team was all together. He looked at the eyes staring at him.

'It's over,' said Macleod. 'She told us about it. Achterberg and she worked together. They didn't know each other from before, but Achterberg went to seek revenge for his daughter, albeit one that he brought into this world by methods that were not the nicest. He also revisited that sin on Paula. I'd like to say to you all, well done for your professionalism, for your effort, and your work. I don't feel like having a celebration now. We might have been quicker,' said Macleod. 'We might have got there. I don't know. But you did your best. It's not your fault.'

He turned and walked off to the kitchenette. Susan went to go after him, but Perry grabbed her arm, shaking his head.

Hope turned to the team and put her hand up. She followed Macleod out to the kitchenette. He was stood with both hands on the sideboard, his head bowed. She could hear the tears flowing. She walked up behind him, put her arms around him, and held him tightly.

'Not your fault,' she said. 'Not your fault.'

'How many years?' he said. 'I know that. I do know that. It doesn't make it any easier.' Macleod continued to weep, almost turning into a wail.

From outside, Perry and the team could hear him. They could hear Hope telling him to just let it go. Susan turned round and wrapped her arms around Perry, and he felt tears of his own flowing to mix with hers. Somebody's lust had cost a young girl her life. A young man, his too. The team knew they would suffer in the next couple of days for it.

Macleod emerged from the kitchenette, Hope following behind him. He looked at the corridor, and at the team standing there.

'Yes,' he said. 'I know.'

'I don't think we should have a celebration,' said Hope. 'But we're tired, we're hungry and we need to eat. In the cars, everyone.'

The team brushed past and Macleod picked up his mobile.

'You're coming,' said Hope.

'I am,' said Macleod. 'I'm just going to call Jane. She'll be wondering. She'll be thinking about me, especially when she finds out that, well, it ended like this.'

'Okay,' said Hope.

Macleod re-entered his office and spent the next five minutes talking to Jane. By the time he got to the car, he'd been to the bathroom and wiped water across his face. He sat in the seat beside Hope as she turned on the engine.

'What do you fancy?' she said. 'Indian, Chinese, Italian, British, Scottish, Paraguayan. You can get me stuff from anywhere.'

'I don't care. I just want to eat.'

She put her hand across onto his. 'Then we eat. The big boss has spoken.'

He gave her a smile. He'd be all right in a few days. Or he'd

be better. When it happened like this, these cases never left
you.

Read on to discover the Patrick
Smythe series!

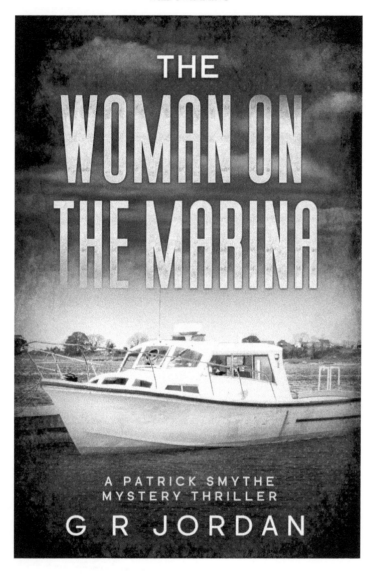

THE

WOMAN ON

THE MARINA

A PATRICK SMYTHE
MYSTERY THRILLER

G R JORDAN

Patrick Smythe is a former Northern Irish policeman who

after suffering an amputation after a bomb blast, takes to the sea between the west coast of Scotland and his homeland to ply his trade as a private investigator. Join Paddy as he tries to work to his own ethics while knowing how to bend the rules he once enforced. Working from his beloved motorboat 'Craigantlet', Paddy decides to rescue a drug mule in this short story from the pen of G R Jordan.

Join G R Jordan's monthly newsletter about forthcoming releases and special writings for his tribe of avid readers and then receive your free Patrick Smythe short story.

Go to https://bit.ly/PatrickSmythe for your Patrick Smythe journey to start!

About the Author

GR Jordan is a self-published author who finally decided at forty that in order to have an enjoyable lifestyle, his creative beast within would have to be unleashed. His books mirror that conflict in life where acts of decency contend with self-promotion, goodness stares in horror at evil, and kindness blindsides us when we at our worst. Corrupting our world with his parade of wondrous and horrific characters, he highlights everyday tensions with fresh eyes whilst taking his methodical, intelligent mainstays on a roller-coaster ride of dilemmas, all the while suffering the banter of their provocative sidekicks.

A graduate of Loughborough University where he masqueraded as a chemical engineer but ultimately played American football, Gary had worked at changing the shape of cereal flakes and pulled a pallet truck for a living. Watching vegetables freeze at -40'C was another career highlight and he was also one of the Scottish Highlands "blind" air traffic controllers.

These days he has graduated to answering a telephone to people in trouble before telephoning other people to sort it out.

Having flirted with most places in the UK, he is now based in the Isle of Lewis in Scotland where his free time is spent between raising a young family with his wife, writing, figuring out how to work a loom and caring for a small flock of chickens. Luckily, his writing is influenced by his varied work and life experience as the chickens have not been the poetical inspiration he had hoped for!

You can connect with me on:
🌐 https://grjordan.com
📘 https://facebook.com/carpetlessleprechaun

Subscribe to my newsletter:
✉ https://bit.ly/PatrickSmythe

Also by G R Jordan

G R Jordan writes across multiple genres including crime, dark and action adventure fantasy, feel good fantasy, mystery thriller and horror fantasy. Below is a selection of his work. Whilst all books are available across online stores, signed copies are available at his personal shop.

The Wrong Man (Highlands & Islands Detective Book 41)
https://grjordan.com/shop/highlands-islands-detective/the-wrong-man
An unresolved murder of Macleod's former colleague. A wall of silence within the ranks to the point of death. Can New DI Emmett Grump pull the blind and lay a thirty-year-old mystery to rest?

Installed by DCI Macleod in the new Inverness cold case unit, DI Emmett Grump must contend with current and former officers who will not talk about a murder over three decades old. Assisted by DS Sabine Ferguson, Grump must shake off the persistent cold shoulder as he finds a cancer within the force hidden for many years. Shunned and mocked, Grump and Ferguson find their own lives threatened as the long-established veil crumbles.

Tread carefully, lest you wake the lion!

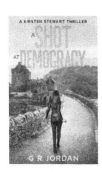

Kirsten Stewart Thrillers
https://grjordan.com/product/a-shot-at-democracy
Join Kirsten Stewart on a shadowy ride through the underbelly of the Highlands of Scotland where among the beauty and splendour of the majestic landscape lies corruption and intrigue to match any city. From murders to extortion, missing children to criminals operating above the law, the Highland former detective must learn a tougher edge to her work as she puts her own life on the line to protect those who cannot defend themselves.

Having left her beloved murder investigation team far behind, Kirsten has to battle personal tragedy and loss while adapting to a whole new way of executing her duties where your mistakes are your own. As Kirsten comes to terms with working with the new team, she often operates as the groups solo field agent, placing herself in danger and trouble to rescue those caught on the dark side of life. With action packed scenes and tense scenarios of murder and greed, the Kirsten Stewart thrillers will have you turning page after page to see your favourite Scottish lass home!

There's life after Macleod, but a whole new world of death!

Jac's Revenge (A Jac Moonshine Thriller #1)

https://grjordan.com/product/jacs-revenge

An unexpected hit makes Debbie a widow. The attention of her man's killer spawns a brutal yet classy alter ego. But how far can you play the game before it takes over your life?

All her life, Debbie Parlor lived in her man's shadow, knowing his work was never truly honest. She turned her head from news stories and rumours. But when he was disposed of for his smile to placate a rival crime lord, Jac Moonshine was born. And when Debbie is paid compensation for her loss like her car was written off, Jac decides that enough is enough.

Get on board with this tongue-in-cheek revenge thriller that will make you question how far you would go to avenge a loved one, and how much you would enjoy it!

A Giant Killing (Siobhan Duffy Mysteries #1)
https://grjordan.com/product/a-giant-killing
A body lies on the Giant's boot. Discord, as the master of secrets has been found. Can former spy Siobhan Duffy find the killer before they execute her former colleagues?

When retired operative Siobhan Duffy sees the killing of her former master in the paper, her unease sends her down a path of discovery and fear. Aided by her young housekeeper and scruff of a gardener, Siobhan begins a quest to discover the reason for her spy boss' death and unravels a can of worms today's masters would rather keep closed. But in a world of secrets, the difference between revenge and simple, if brutal, housekeeping becomes the hardest truth to know.

The past is a child who never leaves home!